"Let's get one thing clear," she said. "What happened was supposed to stay in Vegas. It will *never* happen again."

"Never, huh? That's a long time."

"I'm *serious*. I've worked too hard to get where I am to let some man screw up my life."

He pulled her into his arms and tilted her face up to his.

"I think you know I'm not just 'some man,'" he said as he brushed his lips across hers. "I'm magic."

With that, he deepened the kiss. Their tongues darted and danced and he pulled her closer, wanting more.

He was reaching for the buttons on her blouse when the sharp whistle that signalled the arrival of a text message on his phone blared.

Becky jumped back, staring at him with undisguised horror.

"I'm not sure if you're magic," she whispered. "But I *am* beginning to think you might be the devil."

"I've been called worse by my competition," he said. "But usually not until after I beat them."

Dear Reader

I've worked in the world of advertising for far longer than is healthy. It's a wild and woolly world, filled with beautiful people, strong personalities, and lots and lots of drama.

It is, in other words, the perfect place to set a romance novel.

For a really long time I was too busy living in it to find time to write about it. When inspiration finally did strike it was National Novel-Writing Month (or NaNoWriMo, as those of us insane enough to participate like to call it), and I had thirty days to pound out a fifty-thousand-word novel.

For twenty of those days the words flew through my fingers and on to my computer screen faster than I could speak them. Unfortunately on day twenty-one I discovered I was telling the wrong story. The words stopped, the story stalled, and Mark and Becky took up residence in my head.

They stayed there for almost four years. And, let me tell you, they were obnoxious house guests—always whispering in my ear, trying to get me to write the right story and set them free.

I finally did it last fall, during the *So You Think You Can Write* contest. I didn't win, but Mark and Becky caught the right editor's attention. And now, less than five months later, I'm writing you this letter.

It's been the adventure of a lifetime. A dream come true. And one heck of a relief—Mark and Becky have finally vacated my head.

If you enjoy this story one-tenth as much as I enjoyed writing it you're in for a treat. They're delightful people, living in a delightfully insane world.

Thanks for reading!

Amber

ALL'S FAIR IN LUST & WAR

BY

AMBER PAGE

First published in Great Britain 2014
by Mills & Boon, an imprint of Harlequin (UK) Limited,
Eton House, 18-24 Paradise Road, Richmond, Surrey, TW9 1SR

ISBN: 978-0-263-24296-6

Harlequin (UK) Limited's policy is to use papers that are natural,
renewable ar
sustainable f
to the legal e

Printed and b
by CPI Anto

Amber Page has been writing stories since—well, since she could write, and still counts the pinning of her 'Bubble People' tale to the classroom bulletin board in the third grade as one of her happiest childhood memories.

She's also an avid reader, and has been addicted to romances since she first discovered them on the dusty shelves of her favourite library as a young teen. The nerdy little bookworm she was is still pinching herself to make sure that this whole 'getting published by Mills & Boon®' thing is real.

When not penning Happily-Ever-Afters, Amber works as an advertising writer in the heart of Indiana, where she lives with the love of her life, their daughter, and a menagerie of furry animals. She also blogs, gardens, and sometimes even manages to sneak in a few hours of sleep.

Don't ask her how she does it all. She's too tired to remember.

ALL'S FAIR IN LUST & WAR
is Amber Page's debut book
for Mills & Boon® Modern Tempted™
and is also available in ebook format
from www.millsandboon.co.uk

DEDICATION

To my husband, my biggest cheerleader and occasional butt-kicker. Thank you for refusing to let me give up.

To Allison, Amanda, Christina, Meagan, Rhonda and Tanya, whose speed-reading skills and smart critiques helped make this book what it is.

And to everyone else who cheered me along the way (you know who you are).

PROLOGUE

MARK AWOKE SLOWLY, his mouth fuzzy and his limbs strangely heavy. He rolled over, expecting to see…who? Certainly not the empty pillow that greeted him.

Head spinning slightly, he lifted himself up on his elbow to look around the room. He was in his hotel room, right? Seeing his laptop on the desk, he decided it was probably safe to assume he was still in Vegas and hadn't hopped on a plane to Bangladesh or something.

He kept his gaze moving, noting two wine glasses, a knocked-over bottle of red wine—damn, he hoped they didn't charge him for that stain on the carpet—and there, by the heavy hotel room door, a pair of cheetah-print stilettos.

Suddenly memory came rushing back.

Walking down to the AdWorld closing party. Seeing the pretty blonde in the tight red dress giggling into her phone. Feeling compelled to talk to her. And then—*wham!* Being hit in the gut by a lightning bolt of lust when she turned to grin up at him with her sparkling green eyes.

He would have done anything to get closer to her. To get to know her.

Which was probably why he'd found himself doing something totally out of character.

"I'm Mark," he'd said, taking her hand in his and grazing her knuckles with his lips. "May I have the honor of escorting you this evening, my lady?"

She'd swallowed loudly, and he'd seen the desire sparking in her eyes.

Nonetheless, she'd been as cool as ice when she'd answered him. "I'd love that. Shall we?"

He'd held out his arm for her to take and together they stepped through the ballroom doors into the strobe-lit party beyond.

That had been followed by copious drinking, he was sure. His mind showed him an image of her gazing at him uncertainly before raising a tequila glass.

"Let's toast," she'd said. "To one wild night."

"To one wild, scandalous night," he'd answered.

And there'd been dancing. He remembered how she'd laughed as she spun away, then melted when he drew her close again. And how sweet her lips had tasted when he'd pulled her in for a kiss…

The first of many kisses.

Eventually she'd clung to him and said, "Mark, I can't believe I'm saying this, but I *need* you. Take me back to your room?"

What had followed had been one of the most…no, *the* hottest night of his life.

She'd been so hot, so willing to do anything… And when they'd finished she'd rolled over and said, "Wanna do it again?"

His answer had been, "Hell, yes."

But what was her name again?

Just then the bathroom door opened and she stepped out, engulfed in the hotel-issue robe, her long blond hair dripping down her back. She looked at him and smiled, green eyes sparkling.

The lightning bolt hit home again.

"Becky," he said. Her name was Becky.

"Hey, gorgeous," she said.

"Hey, yourself. What are you doing up so early?"

"Oh," she said, a momentary frown crossing her small face. "My flight leaves in a few hours, and I've got some work to do this morning. I figured I should probably get a move on."

"Ah," he said, overcome with an inexplicable sense of disappointment. "I thought maybe we could go get some breakfast. Or, you know, have breakfast in bed." Which, honestly, had been the last thing on his mind until she'd emerged from the bathroom. But once he'd seen her he'd been able to think of nothing he'd rather do other than peel that giant robe off her tiny frame.

She gave him a pained smile and perched on the edge of the bed.

"I'd love to, but you know how it goes. Duty calls."

Reading her tense body language, Mark realized it was no use. He also knew he wasn't ready to let her go yet. "All right. I understand," he said slowly, seeking a conversational gambit that would keep her talking. "You know, we never even talked about our jobs. What do you do?"

"I'm a copywriter. For an agency in New York—SBD," she said slowly.

"Really? What a coincidence. I'm starting a new gig—"

Gently, she placed her hand over his mouth. "You know what? Don't tell me about you. Last night was—well, it was magical, but I'm not looking to start a relationship. Even a casual one. If you don't mind, I'd just like to think of you as Mark the Magic Man from Las Vegas…not a real person I might run into at the supermarket."

Wow. That was a first. Usually it was *him* trying to duck out while a girl tried to pry information out of him. He wasn't so sure he liked being on this end of things. But his pride wouldn't allow him to admit that to her.

"Hmm," he said. "I kind of like being a Magic Man. Maybe I should go into business."

She threw her head back and laughed, and suddenly the tension eased. Then she leaned forward and kissed him. Hard.

"Thank you for last night. Believe me when I tell you it's one I'll never forget."

He smiled. "Me neither," he said. And he meant it.

Moments later Becky finished getting dressed and, holding her heels in one hand, she blew him a kiss.

"Bye, Magic Man."

"Bye, Gorgeous Girl."

And then she was gone.

"Until tomorrow, then," he said to himself.

Reaching for his iPad, he loaded up the search engine. It was time to look up his gorgeous new coworker.

CHAPTER ONE

BECKY WAS ENGROSSED in the dreary task of sorting through her inbox, attempting to make sense of the three hundred and fifty-seven emails that had accumulated while she was in Vegas, when a cardboard coffee cup was slammed down on her desk.

"One venti dark roast with a splash of vanilla soy milk," Jessie said. "Just the way you like it."

Becky looked up and grinned at her redheaded friend.

"Aw, thanks, Jessie. You didn't have to do that."

Jessie shrugged her coat off, threw it on the visitor's chair, then collapsed at her desk.

"It's bribery. Now, *spill.*"

"Spill? You want me to spill this delicious coffee?"

Jessie threw her rainbow-colored scarf at her. "Don't be an idiot. You know what I want to know. What happened after you texted me Saturday night? Were you able to prove to yourself that your libido isn't dead?"

Becky blushed. "It's alive and kicking," she said. "And very insistent."

"Woo-hoo! My girl scored! I knew you could do it!" Jessie said, grinning. "Now, tell me the juicy bits."

Becky shook her head. "A lady never kisses and tells," she said, laughing.

"Give me a break," Jessie said, rolling her eyes. "I've known you for ten years, and in all that time you've never kept a secret from me. Give it up, sister."

Becky shook her head again. While it was true that she

and Jessie had always told each other everything, this felt different. Special.

"I'm sorry, Jessie. It just doesn't feel appropriate to talk about it here. Besides, you know what they say. What happens in Vegas..."

Just then her boss's voice rumbled from the vicinity of her open office door. "Is supposed to stay in Vegas, right?"

Becky whirled, readying a snappy comeback. But what she saw stopped her in her tracks.

Her boss, David, was standing there, smiling. And with him was...Mark.

Mark? How could Mark be standing in her office? Becky stared at him, mouth open. It was not possible. Completely impossible, in fact.

Mark belonged in Vegas, not in New York City.

Heat flared in her belly as she remembered the last time they'd met. She'd been texting Jessie, trying to find the courage to walk into the closing night party by herself.

Just picture them standing in their underwear...then stalk the guy that makes you drool, Jessie had texted.

"Right. Underwear," she'd said to herself. "Must picture delicious-looking men in underwear."

And that was when she'd heard Mark's rumbling voice for the first time.

"Well, if you're looking for volunteers, I happen to be available."

"What?" she'd yelped, whirling to face the interloper. Then her heart had stopped. The man smiling at her was the living, breathing definition of delicious, from the tips of his artfully rumpled black hair to the toes of his polished leather shoes.

Brilliant white teeth flashed as he grinned down at her. "If you need help. Picturing what a man looks like in his underwear, I mean. I'm happy to serve as a model."

Becky's face flamed. "Oh, I...uh...no one was supposed

to hear that. I just…I was having trouble walking into the party by myself. My friend suggested I picture everyone in their underwear. As, you know, a motivator."

Mr. Gorgeous tilted his head back and laughed, and as he did Becky felt it. The zing. The tingle. If she'd been alone she would have done a happy dance. He'd just proved she wasn't dead inside!

Now that he was standing in her office, she kind of wished she had been.

Becky shook her head to clear it. She needed to pay attention to the conversation that was happening now if she wanted to make sense of the situation.

"Yeah, you're supposed to leave all the juicy details at the airport," Jessie said. "But I was trying to convince Becky to give me some of the gory details anyway."

"Any luck?" asked Mark, giving Becky a sidelong glance.

"None." Jessie pouted.

"Well, I was there," he said. "You didn't miss much. Although the closing night party was unexpectedly awesome."

Becky's head snapped up. Was he teasing her? And, if he was, how dared he? Mark just looked at her with a half smile on his face, his dark eyes glinting mischievously.

"That's what Becky said. Did you two meet?" Jessie asked.

"No!" Becky practically shouted.

"Yeah, you could say that," Mark said at the same time.

Becky stared at him. He said nothing, just quirked one damnably expressive eyebrow at her and leaned back against the doorframe, letting her take the lead.

"Well, what I meant was we didn't really spend much time together," she said.

Just twelve mind-blowing hours and fifty-three bone-melting minutes. Not that she'd been counting or anything.

Her traitorous mind flashed back to their first kiss. The

way he'd claimed every part of her mouth and set her whole body aflame. Within seconds she'd known she wanted more from him than a few kisses.

But it was only supposed to be for one night. If she'd known he'd turn up here she would have never…

"Mark, here, is an amazingly talented art director," her boss said, reaching up to clap him on the back. "I've brought him in on a freelance basis to work on a special project. And I want you to work with him, Becky."

"Me?" she squeaked. "But I'm busy with… I mean, I've got…"

"Whatever you currently have on your plate will be given to someone else," her boss replied. "I need you on this. Be in my office at eleven. We'll talk."

Becky snapped her mouth shut, knowing further protest was useless and foolhardy. When David told you to do something, you did it. At least you did if you wanted to keep your job.

Which she did. Unfortunately.

"Okay," she said. "I'll see you then."

"Good," he answered. "Then I won't keep you any longer. Come on, Mark."

After they were gone Becky put her head down on her desk, banging it lightly against the keyboard.

"Why, universe, *why?* Why would you do this to me?"

"Becky? What's wrong?" Jessie asked.

Becky shook her head mutely.

"Oh, come on, you can tell me. You have to."

Becky knew she was right. If she didn't, her soon-to-be-bizarre behavior wouldn't make much sense. And if there was one person she didn't want to alienate it was Jessie.

Besides, Jessie was the only one who knew what had happened…*before.* And what she had been trying to prove to herself that night in Vegas.

Becky got up to close the door before turning to face

her friend. Blowing her hair off her forehead, she said, "It was him."

"Him? Who? I'm not following," Jessie said.

"Mark. Mark was the man I met in Las Vegas. And things went a little bit further than I had planned."

"What do you mean?"

"I spent the night with him…" Becky groaned.

"Are you kidding me?" Jessie asked, falling back into her chair.

Becky shook her head.

Jessie tilted her head back and howled with laughter.

"Oh, my God. Only you… This is…it's unbelievable."

Becky glared at her. "I really don't think this is funny."

"Of course you don't. But, girl, you gotta believe me when I tell you it is."

Easy for her to say. She wasn't the one living in a nightmare.

Finally Jessie sobered.

"All right, so Mr. One-Night Stand has become Mr. Works Down the Hall. What are you going to do about it?"

"Nothing," Becky said flatly.

"Why? Was it…bad?"

Pictures from their night together flashed through Becky's brain. His lips kissing her mouth. His tongue on her breast. His hands…everywhere.

"It was amazing."

"Did you hit the big O?"

Becky blushed. "Oh, yeah. More than once."

Jessie looked thoughtful. "Then why not see if this could go somewhere? You know—like, casual relationshippy. Fate seems to be telling you it should."

Becky stood up, restless. "You know better than anyone why not. After everything that happened with Pence I'll never have a relationship with someone I work with again."

Jessie came up behind her and hugged her shoulders.

"I understand. But, Becky, that was a long time ago. You were a different person. And he was your boss, not a coworker. Besides, you can't let him ruin your whole life. If you do, he wins."

Sneaking a look at the clock on the wall, she groaned.

"We'll have to talk about this more later, Jessie. I gotta go to the Hall of Doom."

"All right, girl. Knock 'em dead."

Mark wasn't sure how much more of this small talk he could take.

He'd been sitting in David's office for what felt like hours, talking about everything except the reason he was here. He now knew where the bald man's favorite golf course was—South Carolina—what he preferred to drink—bourbon, straight up—and even how he had gotten his name—his mom had named him after Michelangelo's *David.*

But he still didn't know what his first assignment was going to be or why it had to be secret. When David had called him to see if he might be interested he'd said only that he needed help winning a giant piece of new business—one that had the potential to change the future of the agency.

That was interesting enough, but it was what David had said next that had sold him on the job.

"Mark, I've been searching everywhere for someone who can help me bring this home. When your name came up I knew you were the man for the job. I need you on this."

"How did you get my name?" Mark had asked, afraid that it was another one of his stepfather's pieces of charity.

"Mark, you've taken home gold from almost every major advertising competition there is. Your name is everywhere."

Which meant this was a job he'd gotten on his own merits—not through his damned stepfather's connections.

Even better, David had all but promised him a permanent spot in the creative leadership team once they landed the account.

It was the opportunity he'd spent the past ten years working toward. He couldn't wait to get started.

He just wished he knew what Becky had to do with it.

When he'd looked her up, he'd been amazed at how talented she seemed to be. In the five short years she'd been working as a copywriter she'd earned herself numerous awards. The whole reason she'd been in Vegas was because she was being honored with another award—this one for a social-media campaign she'd masterminded that had gone viral.

In short, she was as amazing in the boardroom as she was in the bedroom.

And what he wouldn't give to experience that again!

He remembered how hot she'd looked, standing in his room clad only in her red lace bra and panties. And how much better she'd looked out of them…

Unfortunately the look on her face when she'd found him standing in her office had been completely and utterly horrified—and, if he wasn't mistaken, more than a little bit furious. He didn't think she was having the same kinds of thoughts he was having right now.

Just then there was a soft knock on the door.

"Come in," David said.

The door opened and Becky quietly entered the room.

He wasn't sure how it was possible, but she looked even sexier in her blazer and jeans than she had wearing a cocktail dress.

She flashed a quick look at him, and flushed when he caught her eye. Man, how he'd love to see how far down that flush went.

"Thank you for coming, Becky, my girl," David boomed. Although he couldn't have been much more than forty, the man mimicked the vocal mannerisms of a *Mad Men*–style ad man. "Sit, sit, sit. We have a lot to talk about."

She glided across the thick red carpet and sat primly in the oversize club chair next to Mark.

"I trust you had a good time in Vegas, my dear?" David asked.

Becky seemed to force out a smile. "It was amazing, David. Thank you so much for letting me go."

"Of course—you deserved it. Besides, I knew you were one woman I could trust not to get too carried away in Vegas. I would have never sent that partner of yours. She's trouble with a capital *T*."

Becky's laugh sounded even more forced than her smile had been. "Yeah, you know me. Married to my job and all that."

"Oh, not to worry, Becky. Sooner or later a fine-looking girl like you is bound to get snapped up. Then you'll be too busy having babies to write brilliant campaigns for me anymore. That's how it always goes. Right, Mark?"

Mark was floored. People still talked like *that?* In an *office?* It was a miracle this guy hadn't been slapped with a multimillion-dollar lawsuit yet. Or, judging from the fury flashing in Becky's eyes, murdered.

"I don't know about that, David. I know plenty of working mothers who—"

David cut him off. "Right, right. I know. Girls can do anything men can—blah, blah, blah. None of that matters right now, because my brilliant little sparrow is as single as they come…and I'm going to be keeping you both too busy for her to change matters any."

Becky sucked in a breath and seemed about to say something, but she never got the chance.

"All right. Enough of this chitchat. Let's get down to business, shall we? You two are among the most talented creatives this business has to offer," David said. "And I'm going to need every bit of juice you've got. We've been asked to take part in the agency search for Eden. You both know what that is?"

Becky nodded. "The yogurt company?"

"You got it," David said. "They're coming out with a new line of low-fat, all-natural Greek yogurt flavors designed to get all those pretty hipster ladies hot and bothered. Our job is to figure out how to do that. And, since their advertising budget is a quarter of a billion dollars, we damn well better nail it."

Becky practically bounced up and down in her chair. "Oh, I'd love to get my hands on that one," she said.

"Oh, those pretty little hands are going to be all over it. So are yours, Mark. Just…er…hopefully not on the same spot at the same time!" he said.

Mark laughed uncomfortably. "No chance of that happening, sir." At least not that David needed to know about.

"Good. Now, the Eden people tell me they don't want any 'suits' working on their account. They want something young and fresh…something none of our existing creative directors are. That means you two have the opportunity of a lifetime."

David got up from his chair and started to pace.

"So here's what we're going to do. We're going to break the agency into two creative teams. Becky, you're going to head up one. Mark, you'll be in charge of the other. Whichever one of you comes up with the winning concept and sells it to the client will win a fifty-thousand-dollar bonus—and become the youngest creative director this agency has ever had."

Mark blinked slowly, trying to wrap his head around this new twist. David had never said anything about a competition.

"You're making me compete for the creative director position?" asked Becky, her eyes sparking angrily in an otherwise pale face. "But you told me that when I came back from AdWorld the job was as good as mine!"

"It is," David said. "All you have to do is win the Eden account."

Mark watched as Becky sprang up from her chair. There was no doubt that murder was on her mind.

"I will," she said from between clenched teeth. Then she turned to glare at Mark. "And don't you dare think for a second that you've got a shot!"

With that, she strode from the room, controlled fury in every movement. Good thing he had no problem with beating a sexy woman at her own game, because there was no way he was losing *this* job.

Turning to David, he said, "This competition's going to be quite a challenge."

"I'm counting on you to win," David said. "Don't let me down."

"I won't."

Becky slammed her office door so hard the wall shook.

"Wow. What's up *your* butt?" Jessie asked.

"David," Becky said.

"Ewww, that sounds uncomfortable!" Jessie giggled.

Becky glared at her. "It's not funny," she said. "That stupid blowhard is trying to give away my promotion again."

"The one he swore would be yours after you got back from Vegas?"

"The one and the same." Becky sighed, her heels tapping a staccato tune across the cement floor as she paced.

Jessie grabbed Becky's coat. "All right, you're going to tell me what's happened. But not here. A discussion like this calls for hot-fudge sundaes."

* * *

"You don't have to win this by yourself! You've got your whole team behind you," Jessie said between bites of hot fudge.

"I don't know who's on my team yet," Becky said, picking up her spoon, watching as the melting ice cream dripped back into her bowl. "I could get stuck with anyone."

"Did David lay out any rules when he said the creative department was going to be split in half?"

Becky shook her head.

"Then I vote we make the rules for him," Jessie said, grabbing a pen and paper out of her green velvet purse. "All right. No thinking allowed. Tell me who would be on your dream team."

"You," Becky said slowly.

"Yeah, well, obviously. Who else?"

Becky fell silent and looked out of the window at the busy street outside. Three girls walked arm in arm, laughing and talking as they went. Just then one lone man broke through their line, forcing their arms apart. They let him through, but shot up their middle fingers at him after he passed.

"I know what we need," she said, excitement zinging through her pores. "Jessie, we need girl power. Let's make this a battle of the sexes."

"Wait—what?"

"David thinks women creatives don't have it in them to be as good as men. Let's prove him wrong. Let's gather all the women in the department on our team and let Mark have the men."

"But there are more guys than girls in our department. It won't be an even match," Jessie said.

"Numbers aren't everything," Becky said. "Especially since the product in question is aimed squarely at women our age.'"

Jessie put down her spoon. "You, my dear, are brilliant."

"Well, yeah," Becky said. "Haven't you seen my awards shelf?"

"I have." Jessie snorted. "You think it's bigger than Mark's?"

"Hmm, I don't know," Becky said, her mind showing her wicked images of Mark's thick penis twitching in her palm as she kissed his muscled chest. "I honestly don't know much about him at all. Other than the fact that he's magic…"

"Magic?"

Becky started, reluctantly letting her daydream disappear.

"That's what I told him he was. Magic Man from Vegas."

Jessie stared at her, her blue eyes almost green with jealousy. "Man, that must have been one good night."

"The best," Becky said. Seeing the question in Jessie's eyes, she put her hand up in a "stop" gesture. "But it was just one night. I don't want or need a man in my life right now. What I need," she said, grinning, "is a team of Magic Women. Let's go put it together."

"I *knew* my girl was in there somewhere. And—" Jessie grinned, handing Becky the check "—since you're about to be fifty thousand dollars richer, I'll let you get this."

Becky rolled her eyes. "Fine," she said. "But only because you're about to work your ass off for me."

Mark was staring out through the window of his office at the crowds teeming past on Madison Avenue, wondering what on earth he had gotten himself into.

Usually he was brought in to save the day. Agencies never called him until they were facing a problem they couldn't solve—a challenge they couldn't meet. He got to play the part of vagabond hero. He came in, slayed the dragon, claimed a few hot nights with the delicious advertising damsels he had rescued, then left.

He didn't get to know the other players in the story. Never bothered to worry about whose toes he was stomping on, or what effect his actions had on those left behind when he rode off into the sunset.

His life, both professional and personal, was very much a case study in the "Wham, Bam, Thank You, Ma'am," approach to life. And that was the way he liked it.

After all, the one and only time he'd allowed himself to fall in love he'd found out the hard way that it had been his stepfather's name—or, more aptly, his money—that had gotten him the girl. And when she'd found out that Mark would never inherit the family fortune Sandra had turned to someone who *did* have top billing on a rich man's will.

The day he'd found Sandra in bed with his stepbrother hadn't been the first time he'd cursed his stepfamily, but it had been the last time he'd admitted to being part of it.

These days he didn't need anybody or anything. Well, nothing except for a killer job and a place among advertising's greats—a place he'd earned on his own.

So why did a certain blonde keep interrupting his thoughts?

Just then Becky strode in, fire in her eyes.

"Wow, hey—thanks for knocking," he said, trying to ignore the way his pulse quickened when she entered the room.

She stalked forward until she was standing directly in front of him. She took a long, slow look around the room and he knew she must be taking in the overly plush carpet, richly upholstered furnishings, the floor-to-ceiling windows and comparing it with her own small if brightly colored closet.

"Nice setup," she said. "What'd you do? Sleep with David to get it?"

He snorted. "I think you know that's not the way my tastes run, babe."

Her face flushed, and he would have given anything to know what she was thinking. She looked up at him and he could see the heat veiled behind her professional fury.

"Let's get one thing clear," she said. "What happened was supposed to stay in Vegas, just like David said. It will *never* happen again."

"Never, huh? That's a long time."

She looked away quickly, but not before he saw the desire flashing in her eyes.

"I'm *serious,*" she said, folding her arms across her chest. "I've worked too hard to get where I am to let some man screw up my life again."

The disdain in her voice struck deep. So she thought she could just dismiss the maddening attraction that raced between them, huh? It was time to prove her wrong.

He pulled her into his arms and tilted her face up to his, giving in to the urge he'd been fighting since she'd walked into the room.

"I think you know I'm not just 'some man,'" he said, as he brushed his lips across hers. "I'm magic."

With that, he deepened the kiss. For a second she stiffened, but then something in her seemed to give. With a soft moan, she relaxed against him and opened her mouth.

He lost himself in the chocolate-flavored cavern as hunger roared to life. Their tongues darted and danced and he pulled her closer, wanting more.

He was reaching for the buttons on her blouse when the sharp whistle that signaled the arrival of a text message on his phone blared.

Becky jumped back, staring at him with undisguised horror.

"I'm not sure if you're magic," she whispered. "But I am beginning to think you might be the devil."

Mark took a breath, shaken by how fast he had lost control. Obviously the heat that had sparked between them in Vegas had been no fluke.

"I've been called worse by my competition," he said. "But usually not until after I beat them."

She briefly closed her eyes, and when she opened them again her stare was fiercely competitive.

"Right. The competition. I came to tell you that I've chosen my team. I'll take the women—you take the men."

"A battle of the sexes, huh? All right, if that's the way you want to play it," he said, still trying to get himself under control.

"No, that's the way I plan to *win* it," she said. "I never lose."

"Neither do I, Gorgeous Girl," Mark said, getting angry. "But guess what? One of us is going to. And it won't be me."

She took a deep breath and straightened her spine.

"Yes. It will. This job is mine and there's no way I'm going to let you steal it," she growled, then strode from the room.

"I'm not going to steal it. I'm going to earn it," he said to her departing back.

And he would. He just hoped he didn't have to crush her in the process.

CHAPTER TWO

BECKY LOOKED AT the team gathered around the tempered glass conference table. All eight women in the SBD creative department were looking at her expectantly.

"Raise your hand if David has ever belittled your abilities," she said.

Eight hands shot into the air.

"That's what I thought. Now, raise your hand if you'd like a chance to prove that chauvinist pig wrong."

Again hands shot into the air, this time accompanied by hoots and hollers.

Becky smiled. "Good. Today's your lucky day, ladies. We're going to win a two-hundred-and-fifty-million-dollar piece of business—and we're going to do it without the help of a single man."

Her crew burst into spontaneous applause.

"Now, let's get down to business. Cheri. What do you think of when I say delicious low-fat Greek yogurt?"

"Um…breakfast?" the brunette answered.

Becky turned to the whiteboard and wrote "BREAKFAST" in caps.

"Good. What else? Tanya?"

"Healthy."

Becky wrote it down.

"What else? Anyone?"

"A shortcut to skinny," Jessie said.

"Oh, I like that," Becky said, writing it down and underlining it. "Let's explore that."

"Not just skinny. Strong," someone else said. "Because it's got lots of protein in it."

"Popeye!" Tanya said.

Becky laughed. And then inspiration struck.

"Forget Popeye. This yogurt is for Olive Oyl. It's Olive's secret weapon for kicking Popeye's ass!" she said.

The women around the table laughed.

"Now we're on to something," Jessie said. "Here—give me the marker."

Becky handed it over and Jessie drew a ripped Olive Oyl, flexing her guns, one foot resting on top of a prone Popeye.

"Eden Yogurt. For the super-heroine in you," Jessie wrote.

Becky stepped back with a grin on her face, feeling the giddy high that always struck during a good brainstorming session.

"Ladies, we *are* on to something here. Really on to something. Something no guy would think of. So let's make sure they can't steal it. Tanya, do you know where there's any black paper?"

She nodded.

"Great. Go get it. We're going to make ourselves a good old-fashioned, women-only fort!"

A short while later all the conference windows were blocked off with thick black paper.

Jessie handed Becky the sign she'd made. It read, "Women at Work. No Boys Allowed" in pink glitter.

Becky skipped over to the door, tape in hand. She was just about to stick it up when she saw Mark approach. Opening the door, she waggled her sign at him.

"We've already come up with an idea that's going to kick the ass of anything you can come up with," she said, and grinned.

"Oh, really? Then why all the secrecy?" he asked with a raised eyebrow.

"Well, you're already in the boys' club. We thought it only fair that we create a girls' club with an equally exclusionary policy."

"I'll have you know I don't take part in any boys-only activities. I far prefer the company of women."

"Well, right now the women of this agency do not want your company. So go play with the boys. We'll let you back in after we beat you and all your testosterone-addled buddies."

He sighed. "Becky, Becky, Becky. How many times do I have to tell you? You can't beat me. I'm magic."

She sighed in return. "Mark, Mark, Mark. How many times do I have to tell you? You can't beat us. Talent beats magic every time."

"You go ahead and believe that," he said. "But soon you'll be kissing up to your new boss."

"Nope," she said. "Soon you'll be kissing this." And she slapped her denim-clad rear.

"You'd like that," he said.

"I would. Especially if you did it while I was booting your butt out of the office," she said, slamming the door.

He didn't need to know how very much she would love to kiss every inch of his magnificent body—and to have him kiss hers in return. Again.

She would beat him and then he'd be gone, taking his career-endangering sexual magnetism with him.

She had to. If she didn't she'd be lost forever.

Mark sat behind his heavy oak desk, the eerie white light of his monitor providing the only break in the darkness.

He was trying to polish an ad layout, but every time he turned his attention to the screen Becky's mocking face filled it.

Accusing him of being in the boys' club was pretty rich. Truth was, he didn't have a single close friend—in fact, he didn't have *any* male friends. Not real ones, anyway. The last time he'd had a best friend he'd been in sixth grade. His mom had still been single and they'd still been coexisting fairly peacefully, even if she'd never stopped moaning about how tough it was to be a single parent.

Then Bill had entered their lives, and everything had gone down the toilet.

Mark called up Facebook and scanned his friends list, searching for the familiar name. It didn't take long. He clicked onto Tom's profile, telling himself he was just curious. Not lonely.

Tom's page was filled with pictures of his goofy grinning kids and the short, plump brunette who had married him. He wasn't rich. Or particularly successful. But he did seem happy.

Mark leaned back in his chair and sighed. If things had been different—if he'd stayed in the working-class neighborhood where he'd been born instead of being forced to move into the frigidly upper-class world his mom had married into, where nothing mattered more than money—would he have a life like Tom's?

Would he have a wife? Kids?

Unbidden, an image of Becky holding a baby popped into his head. Feeling a sharp pang of panic, he shook his head to clear it. He didn't want a wife or kids. All he had to do was picture Sandra on the day she'd married his stepbrother to remind himself that the only kind of marriage that worked was one based on money. And he was hardly sugar daddy material.

All he needed was a distraction. Pulling out his phone, he scanned his contacts for one of his favorite sex buddies. A little sexting would straighten him right out.

* * *

Becky stood in front of the big laser printer in the central creative area, hands on hips. All her senses were on high alert. She was printing out her team's latest concepts and she didn't want anyone from the opposing side to get a glimpse.

Fortunately it was quiet in the agency. Most of the office doors were closed, and those stuck in the wall-less cube maze were plugged into their headphones. The only sounds were the click-clacking of keyboards and the occasional muffled curse word.

Finally the printer started to hum. Becky took another quick look around, but saw no movement.

She relaxed her guard, pulling out her phone to take a quick peek at her Twitter feed. She'd lost all track of what was going on outside the advertising bubble she lived in.

Suddenly she heard paper shuffling behind her. She whirled just in time to see Mark snatching her ads off the printer.

"Hey, give those back!" she snapped, reaching for the papers in his hand.

"In a minute," he said, turning his back on her. "But not before I see what you're working on."

"That's none of your business," she said, making another grab for them.

"That's what you think," he said, then strode off down the hall with her printouts.

Swearing silently to herself, she hurried after him, hoping with every fiber of her being that no one was watching them. She didn't need her team to see how easily the other side had managed to outwit her.

Once he reached his office he sat down on the front of his desk, still staring thoughtfully at her designs. She slammed the door, then launched herself at him.

"Give. Them. Back," she said, trying to snatch them from him.

He easily deflected her attack, then surprised her by pulling her against him. She went still as she registered his closeness, the heat emanating from his body putting her nerves on high alert.

Damn, he smelled good. Like grass and clean air with a hint of musk.

"Just chill out," he said, from somewhere over her left ear. "I'm not going to steal your ideas. I've got plenty of my own. I just wanted to sneak a peek."

Forcing herself out of the hormone-induced fog his presence induced, Becky pulled away. How was it possible to be so attracted to someone so infuriating?

"Fine," she said, holding her hand out. "You've had your peek. Hand 'em over."

He did, looking at her with a strangely intense expression.

"Don't you want to know what I think?"

Of course she did. "No."

"Well, I'll tell you anyway. I think they're pretty awesome."

"Oh." That wasn't what she had expected him to say. "Really?"

He nodded. "It's a really original idea. One I never would have come up with. The only thing is..."

Instantly anger sparked in her brain. Of course he couldn't let the compliment ride. Men never could. "The only thing is *what?*"

"Hey, don't get mad. I was just going to say that you might try to push the design. The copy carries it, but I think your art directors could give you more."

She looked down at the ads in her hands. He was right. She'd been thinking the same thing.

"Thank you for the advice. But I think we're doing just fine. Jessie is killing herself for me."

"Suit yourself." He shrugged.

She nodded and turned to leave.

"Don't you want to see what we've got going on?"

She stopped. "You're willing to show me?"

"Sure. Fair's fair. But you'll have to look at them on screen. I haven't printed them out yet."

Wow. A man playing fair. That was a first.

She padded across to his computer, prepared to hate whatever she saw. But when she saw what he was working on she couldn't help but smile. This guy sure seemed to know women.

"This is good," she said. "Funny. But..."

"But what?"

"It's just the headline. It's a little too much. Too smug. Tell your copywriter to dial it back a little."

He nodded. "I was thinking the same thing. Thanks."

She headed back to the door, but stopped before she turned the knob. No need to leave on too much of a friendly note.

"I'm still going to beat you," she said.

"Keep dreaming," he retorted.

"Oh, I will." She smiled. "But no matter how good my dreams are, the reality will be even better."

Becky sat staring at her blank computer screen, exhaustion beating at the backs of her eyelids with every blink of the cursor. It was eleven-thirty p.m. on Thursday, and although her team was giving her their all she still worried that it wouldn't be enough.

Three days just wasn't enough time. Not when there was a quarter of a billion dollars on the line.

As tired as she was, she couldn't keep the memories from invading. Couldn't keep from hearing the sneering voice telling her she'd never get anywhere without him. That she was a hack, and always would be. That the only way she'd ever attain any success would be if she kept warming his bed…

A gentle hand clasped her shoulder.

"Hey, space cadet? Did you hear a word I just said?" Jessie asked.

Becky blinked, shaking her head to clear it.

"No, I…"

"You were listening to the mini-Pence in your head again, weren't you?" she said, sympathy plain in her bright blue eyes.

Becky forced a halfhearted smile. "What? Of course not. How could I when I'm surrounded by such a fantastic group of talented women?"

Jessie snorted. "Liar. When was the last time you slept?"

Becky thought for a second. She honestly couldn't remember.

"I can tell by your silence that it's been too long. Go home. Rest. You need to bring your A game tomorrow. It's D-day, you know."

As if she could forget.

"I know. I'll go soon, I promise."

Jessie gave her a long look. Becky could tell she wanted to say something else.

"Really. I will. Don't worry about me."

"All right," Jessie said. "Well, I'm heading out. And I'm taking mini-Pence with me. You don't need *him* being a backseat driver."

This time Becky smiled for real.

"You're right. I don't. Get him out of here, and good riddance."

After Jessie had left Becky headed for the kitchen, and the free coffee that awaited her there. As she waited for her mug to fill with the magic brew she laid her head on the cool metal of the stainless steel countertop and closed her eyes. Just for a second…

Next thing she knew a big hand was shaking her awake. She bolted upright, trying to get her bearings.

"I'm on it, Pence. Don't worry. I just…" she blurted, her mind still in dreamland.

"Hey, it's all right. There's no Pence here. It looks like you just drifted off for a second," a familiar voice said.

Becky blinked. Sure enough, Mark was standing there, smiling gently at her. And in his hand was the cup of coffee she'd been waiting for.

"Here. It's still hot," he said, handing it to her.

She took it silently, waiting for him to comment on what he'd heard her say. He didn't disappoint her.

"Who's Pence?"

She looked at him, expecting to see ridicule in his eyes. But there was only compassion.

"He's the reason I don't do workplace relationships. Or relationships at all, for that matter."

"Ah. Why?"

Without knowing why, Becky found herself wanting to confide in him.

"He was creative director at the agency where I interned during grad school. He was my mentor, and then he became…more. Much more."

That was the understatement of the year. But Mark didn't need to know how bad things had gotten—or how far she'd run to get away from him.

She shrugged her shoulders. "The whole thing left a bad taste in my mouth. So I decided to focus on my career instead. And now here we are. Competing for the promotion that should be mine."

Mark smiled ruefully and lifted his coffee mug. "Indeed we are. Although I have to admit I'd rather be competing to see how fast we can make each other come."

Becky raised an eyebrow. "You don't want this job?"

"Of course I do," he said with a heated smile. "And I'm going to get it. But I'd also like to hear you screaming my name again. Creating killer ads makes me hot."

Becky couldn't stop the laugh that bubbled up. "Well, that's nice to know. But I'm afraid I can't help you. I've got an equally hot campaign to finish."

Mark slowly got out of his chair and walked over to where she stood. "Okay, but just so you know, I'll be thinking about you," he said, dropping a kiss on her neck.

Her blood sizzled at his touch, and she found herself hoping he'd keep going.

Instead he turned and walked away. "Sweet dreams," he called.

Grabbing her still-warm coffee cup from the counter, Becky started the trek back to her office. Sleep would have to wait. She had a campaign to perfect—and a devil of a man to vanquish.

Mark took a deep breath, straightened his black sport coat, and walked into the crowded conference room. He had timed his entrance carefully, so that he was almost late but not quite. He needed every tool in his arsenal to keep Becky off balance.

"Nice of you to show up!" David boomed.

"I was just putting the finishing touches on our concept," Mark answered. "Nothing less than perfection will do, after all."

"That's what I like to hear," David said. "Now, since you're so sure of yourself, how about you go first?"

Mark took a deep breath, then snuck a look at Becky. She was sitting quietly at one end of the giant conference table, her emerald-green dress the only bright spot in the overly industrial room.

She looked at him mockingly. "Yes, Mark, why don't you go first? We're dying to hear what you've come up with."

Mark looked at her, then looked at David.

David nodded encouragingly.

He took a deep breath as he strode to the head of the table. *This is it,* he told himself. *Time to knock their socks off.*

"I've spent a fair bit of time around women," he said. "I like to think I know what makes them tick. In fact," he said, turning to write on the whiteboard behind him, "the way I see it, women want three things… First, they want to look good. Which, for most women, means being skinny. Second, they want other women to be jealous of them. And third," he said, writing the number three with a flourish, "they want a man. Not only that, they want a man of their choosing. And they want him to drool over them. Which, if we're honest, brings us back to number one. But there are plenty of yogurts promising to make women skinny. To stand out, we need to say something different."

He turned the first board over, so the whole room could see a woman in a cocktail dress being admired by a host of attractive men. Once he was sure they'd seen it, he read them the headline.

"'Eden. The yogurt for the woman who knows what she wants.' That's our tagline. We'll use it in connection with women in all kinds of situations. At the beach," he said, flipping over boards sequentially, "in the dressing room, hailing a cab. In every scene men will be staring, open-mouthed, at the female."

When he'd finished a momentary silence filled the room. He glanced from one face to another but couldn't read what anyone was thinking. This crew would be awesome at poker.

Finally he looked at Becky and cocked an eyebrow at

her. The concept had come a long way since the last time she'd seen it.

She cleared her throat.

"So your message is pretty much: 'Eat this, be skinny, get men to lust over you'?" she asked.

He shrugged his shoulders. "In a nutshell. It's taking the bikini-clad woman in a beer commercial and turning it on its head. *Men* get to be the hangers-on."

"Huh… But what about women who aren't interested in men?"

Mark turned to look at her, expecting to see spite in her eyes. But instead he saw genuine interest. "That's a good point," he said. "But I think this idea has legs. It could cover different topics."

She walked around the room, grabbed the marker out of his hand and began to write down ideas. "Like instead of men it could be openmouthed business associates admiring her. Or cyclists left in her dust."

"Oh, I see where you're going," he said. "That could be cool."

She grinned at him, and for the first time since they'd returned to New York he got a glimpse of the happy, gorgeous girl he'd shared a night with in Vegas.

He grinned back. "So, what if—?"

David cleared his throat.

"I like where this is going—but, Becky, didn't you have a concept to present, as well? This *is* a competition," he said.

Becky blinked, and the laughter in her eyes disappeared.

"Right. Of course. Mark, can you clear your stuff out of the way? I'll grab my boards."

A few moments later Becky took center stage. And when she did she was magnetic.

"So, on my team we got to thinking about what women really want. And we think it goes deeper than just being skinny or attracting the right man. That's what our mothers wanted. But we want more. We want to be recognized as the strong, independent beings we are. We want the superhuman feats we accomplish every day to be recognized. After all, today's woman works like a dog at her corporate job, putting in twice as much effort for half the pay, then heads to the gym to ensure she stays model-thin, then goes home to run a household. Today's women are incredible. We think it's time for a marketer to sit up and acknowledge that."

Then she flipped a board over.

It showed a business-suited woman standing in a superhero pose on top of a conference table as her colleagues clapped.

"'You save your world every day before lunch. Choose the only yogurt high-powered enough to keep up with you,'" she said.

She flipped more boards. One of a soccer mom pulling a dirt-covered boy from a vat of quicksand. One of a runner flying ahead of the pack, cape billowing out behind her. And another of a lab-coated woman punching an oversize germ in the mouth so her patients could get away.

After she presented the last board she looked up and smiled. "Every woman deserves to feel like a superhero. Because she *is* one."

Her team applauded.

Mark had to stop himself from joining in.

David looked at Mark, seeming to be waiting for something. Oh. Right. He was supposed to be shooting holes in her concept.

"What about all those young hipsters who don't feel like they're accomplishing anything yet?" he asked.

"Well, we could have smaller situations. A woman stopping a cab before it can get away," she said.

"Or wowing a crowded club with her dance moves?" he suggested.

"Or saving a cat from a snarling dog?" she chimed in.

"Or what about—?"

"I hate to break this up, but we're not in a brainstorming session," David broke in. "We're supposed to be making a decision about which concept to present to the client."

Mark snapped his mouth shut. *Damn it*. He'd gone from shooting her down to making her case for her.

Thinking fast, he smirked in David's direction. "I think the choice is clear," he said. "Superheroes are great—if you're seven. I think most women would rather fantasize about a good-looking man than dress up in a Spandex suit."

The look Becky shot him was murderous. But before she could open her mouth David held up his hand.

"You have a point, Mark," he said. "But there's something in Becky's idea, too. Let me think for a minute. Everybody be quiet."

Instantly the conference room was deathly quiet.

David moved to the front of the room. "Mark, put your boards back up."

"Sure," he said, reaching for them.

"Just do it. Don't talk about it," David snapped.

Mark blinked, then did as he was told. This man could give any dictator a run for his money.

David paced back and forth, picking up boards, shuffling the order, then shuffling them again. After what seemed like an eternity, he finally spoke.

"All right. Here's what we're going to do. I want you to merge these campaigns. They both have their good points, but together they'd be stronger. So," he said, smiling broadly at Mark and Becky, "I want the two of you to work together."

Shocked, Mark stared at Becky.

She stared back, panic in her eyes.

"Together?" she blurted. "But we were competing."

"Not to worry," David said, patting her on the shoulder. "You still are. We'll just have to think of a different way to evaluate you. From now on consider yourselves partners as well as competitors."

CHAPTER THREE

DAVID'S WORDS ECHOED in the now silent room.

"Partners?" Becky squeaked.

David looked at her, a frown working its way between his piercing blue eyes. "That's what I said."

The whole idea was insane. How could they possibly get anything done when they were both focused on winning the competition? Plus, it meant spending a lot of time alone together. Too much time.

"This is a lot of work," she said. "How are Mark and I supposed to get it done without the help of our teams?"

"Well, Becky," David said, looking at her with more than a little disdain, "if you want to be a creative director at this agency you're going to have to learn to be resourceful. Figure it out."

Mark cleared his throat.

"I don't see any reason why the teams can't help us blow the campaign out after we've finalized the concept," he said.

David clapped him on the back. "Now, *that's* the way a creative director thinks. Becky, pay attention to this guy. You could learn a thing or two from him."

As Becky seethed, David gave his full attention to Mark. "You two have the weekend to get this nailed down. I expect you in my office at nine a.m. sharp on Monday morning to present it to me. Any questions?"

Mark looked over the top of the bald man's head at Becky. "You?"

She had plenty of questions. Like, why was David such

a Neanderthal? What did he see in Mark? Why the hell had she decided to be a copywriter, anyway? Surely there were better ways to make a living. Picking up the city's garbage, for example.

But neither of the men in the room could provide the answers, so instead she just shook her head.

"All right. I'll leave you to it," David said. "Jessie, would you come with me to my office, please?"

The redhead nodded and followed him from the room. Everyone else followed her lead, and soon they were alone.

Becky collapsed in one of the deliberately uncomfortable metal chairs. "Now what?"

"Now you let me take you to dinner," Mark said.

Good Lord. The man never let up.

"Dinner? No. We might be partners, but we don't have to be friends."

"Who said anything about being friends? This is just dinner. You gotta eat, right?"

He looked at her with that damn eyebrow quirked and she felt her resolve melting. She *was* hungry. And they had a lot of work ahead of them. It made sense to fuel up before they got started.

"All right. Dinner. But I'll pay. And I'll choose the place."

"You've got a deal," he said, smiling triumphantly.

"Good. Meet me downstairs in fifteen minutes," she said.

That gave her time to come up with a game plan for winning the promotion…and keeping her clothes on this weekend.

Mark paced in front of the glass doors that marked the entrance to SBD, dodging tourists with every turn.

He'd arrived at the designated spot on time. Unfortunately Becky was nowhere in sight. Just like a woman, he found himself thinking. Probably trying to figure out how big his bank account was. Then he caught himself. Where had *that* come from?

Surely David couldn't be rubbing off on him already?

Just then Becky burst through the doors. The killer green dress was gone. In its place was a pair of worn-looking jeans and a baggy rust-colored sweater. And *damn* if she didn't look just as good.

"There you are," he said. "Where are we off to, chief?"

She looked up at him and he noticed her face was scrubbed free of makeup. Without it, she looked all of nineteen.

"That's for me to know and you to find out," she said. "Come on."

He followed her as she wound her way through the congested city streets, ignoring the pressing crowds as only a seasoned New Yorker could.

"So, are you from here?" he asked.

She seemed to hesitate before answering. "No. But I like to pretend that I am."

He wasn't sure what to make of that statement, so he ignored it. "Then where *are* you from?"

"Detroit," she said shortly.

"Ah. Where the weak get killed and eaten, huh?"

"Or pushed to the end of the unemployment line," she said. Then, seeming to realize that she was being rude, she smiled up at him. "How 'bout you? Where's your magic come from?"

"Oh, here and there," he said. "I moved around a lot." From boarding school to summer camp to anywhere else his mother had been able to think of sending him that kept him far from home.

Looking around, he realized they were standing at the corner of Fifty-Third and Sixth. Tourist central.

"Hungry for some overpriced deli sandwiches?" he asked.

"Nope. Just spicy deliciousness," she said, pointing to a food cart.

"Really?"

"Don't look so surprised. It's the best halal cart in town. And it's cheap."

A few minutes later, when they were seated on a bench with their plastic containers on their laps, he had to admit that she knew what she was talking about.

"This is good," he said between bites of lamb and rice. "I wouldn't have pegged you for a street food kind of girl."

"Really? What do I seem like? A steak and champagne enthusiast?" she said with a sarcastic grin.

"No, more like a vegan foodie."

She snorted. "We don't have vegan foodies in the Midwest. Just a bunch of overweight carnivores."

"So what brought you here? To New York?"

Her expression closed. "The bright lights and big agencies, of course. Just like everybody else."

She took a big bite of lamb and rice, then abruptly steered the conversation back to him.

"So. In all your moving around you never made it to the Midwest?"

"Nope. I have an aversion to corn fields."

"Where did you live, then?"

"Well, I lived in New Jersey until I was ten," he said, hoping that would be enough to satisfy her.

"And then…?"

Man, was she persistent. He sighed.

"And then my mom married a rich man and moved to Connecticut."

"Didn't you go with her?"

He laughed bitterly.

"Well, I had a room in her house. But I wasn't really welcome there. She was too busy with her new family. I spent most of my teen years seeing how many boarding schools I could get thrown out of."

Her eyes went round. "Why?"

Thanks to the years of therapy his mom had forced him to do, he knew it was because acting out had been the only thing that got his mother's attention. But he wasn't going to tell Becky that.

Instead, he shrugged. "Why does a teenage boy do anything? But I saw a lot of the East Coast. Massachusetts, New Hampshire, Maine…everywhere fancy pants rich people live."

Becky snorted. "I would have hated you when I was a teenager—you know that?"

He looked at her, genuinely surprised. "Why do you say that?"

"I was the kid doing extra credit projects and sucking up to teachers, hoping they'd help me when it was time to apply for college. I thought kids like you were idiots."

"And what kind of kid was that?"

She looked at him, her eyes flashing with remembered anger.

"Kids who spent all their time screwing around, knowing they could buy their way into college even if their grades sucked. You would have been one of the people making my life miserable because I couldn't afford to waste my time partying with you."

He sat silently for a long minute, unsure of what to say. She was probably right. After his mom had married Bill money had lost all real value. No matter how much he'd charged to his stepfather's accounts, or how outrageous the purchase, no one had blinked an eye. Except…

"Not me. I went to all-boys schools. Girls were rare and always appreciated, no matter how geeky. Besides," he said, brushing her hair back from her face, "even if you were a nerd, I'm sure you were a gorgeous nerd. I would have been just as desperate to get in your pants then as I am now."

She rolled her eyes, looking pleased nevertheless.

"Whatever," she said, looking down at her phone screen. "Whoa. It's almost seven already. What do you say we go back and get our war room set up? That way we can start fresh in the morning."

"That's a good plan. You're just going to move your stuff into my office, right?"

Becky froze. "I…uh…thought we should set up shop someplace public. With more space, I mean. Like, you know, the conference room."

"Why? Are you afraid to be alone with me?" Mark asked, half hoping that she was. He'd love to know he had that kind of power over her.

"What? No. Of course not. I just thought we might need the whiteboards or something," she said, pointedly not looking at him.

"I've got plenty of whiteboards in my office," he said. "I don't know about you, but I like a little privacy when I'm working hard. And everybody can see into the conference room."

She picked at her fingernails. "I don't know…"

He couldn't resist the urge to tease her.

"I promise to be on my best behavior. I won't show you my underwear even if you ask me to."

Becky laughed at his reference to the first time they'd met.

"Okay. Deal. I won't show you mine if you don't show me yours," she said. "But you'll have to help me move my stuff."

By the time they'd finished moving her desk, laptop dock and giant monitors, dark had fallen and the lights from the skyscrapers that surrounded them twinkled like stars.

Becky gazed out of the window and sighed.

"I could get used to a view like this," she said.

Mark came to stand beside her. "It is pretty sweet. Definitely beats the view I had at my last office."

"Oh? Where was that?"

"Los Angeles," he said.

"Oh. Yeah… I can see how you'd get tired of looking at palm trees and bikini-clad babes," Becky teased.

"I was a contract worker. Which meant I was one small step away from sitting in the basement with a red stapler. The only thing I had to look at was fuzzy cubicle walls."

"Ah. At least I'll always have Ryan Gosling to keep me company," she said, motioning to the poster she'd tacked to the wall by her desk.

"If you get tired of looking at him I'm happy to pose for pictures," Mark said.

Becky stepped back. "Now you want to be my eye candy, huh?"

"Nope. I just want you to want me to take my shirt off."

If he only knew… But she wouldn't. She wouldn't even kiss him—at least not again. That morning in his office had been an aberration.

"Dream on, buddy. I don't sleep with the competition."

"I know, I know," he said. "But you can't blame a guy for trying. You know, if you slept with me I might not try so hard to win."

"Yeah, right. I'm pretty sure you don't give up that easily," she said, giving him a sideways smile.

Then she turned away. It was either that or give in to the temptation to rub her hands over the hard planes of his chest.

"I'm going to check my email and then head out for the night," she said. "You?"

"I think I'm just going to head out," he answered. "I

need to hit the hay so I'm ready to rock tomorrow. See ya in the morning."

Becky waved vaguely in his direction as he left and fired up her laptop. She didn't really need to check her email—that was what smartphones were for. But she did need some time to get used to her new surroundings and wrap her head around the situation.

Truth really was stranger than fiction. If she'd set out to write a book she'd never have come up with anything as screwy as this. It was almost reality-show-worthy.

She could see it now: *Flung: Where One-Night Flings Compete.*

Giggling, she peeked at her inbox. She was surprised to see it was flooded with messages of support from the whole creative team. The guy in charge of the agency might be a sleaze, but he sure did hire good people.

She was just about to close it up when she saw a name that froze her heart.

Pence.

What did *he* want?

She considered deleting the email without reading the message, but knew that was the coward's way out. Taking a deep breath, she clicked on his name, willing herself to stay calm.

Hey Babe
Saw you at AdWorld, but I knew you wouldn't want to talk to me so I didn't say hello. Couldn't stop thinking about you, though. You look good. Done good, too. I'd like to say I'm surprised, but you learned from the best—me.
Did you know my agency is pitching to Eden, too? I'd say may the best man win, but we both know who that is—me. I'm sorry I'm going to have to crush you. But, hey, there'll always be a job waiting for you here! Oh, and Chelsea hit the road, so there's a room for you, too.
Pence

Becky read it twice, unable to believe what she was seeing. Unfortunately the message only got more infuriating the second time around.

Could the man be any more repulsive? Was he really inviting her to take his wife's…er…his *ex*-wife's place over email?

Unable to contain her rage, Becky screamed. Her shriek echoed in the mostly empty office, carrying her pain right back to her ears.

She slammed her laptop shut and got up to pace.

There was no reason this should affect her so much. She'd outgrown him. Outstripped him. She was twice as good as that scum-sucker had ever been on his best day.

Seeking confirmation, she grabbed one of her awards off her desk, stroking the golden statue. She was good. *Damn* good. And nothing that man could say would convince her otherwise.

But still she heard the echoes in her brain. "No-good hack," they spat. "Bed-hopping social climber," they hissed. "As terrible on paper as you are in bed," they screamed.

Unable to help herself, Becky chucked the award across the room. It landed with a dull thud, the thick red carpet seeming to reach up to protect it from damage.

Becky caught the sob before it could escape from her throat. It was time to go home.

Becky turned the key in the faded red door that marked the entrance to her third-floor walk-up and trudged up the stairs.

This morning she had felt so confident. So alive. She'd been sure that the world was hers to conquer.

Now? Now all she wanted was a giant glass of wine and the oblivion that came with sleep.

Without bothering to flip on the light switch, Becky stepped into the kitchen and opened the tiny fridge. Wincing at the glaring light, she pulled the Pinot Grigio from the top shelf and took a swig straight from the bottle.

A cockroach scuttled across the bloodred countertop directly opposite her. Without thinking, she slammed the bottle down, reveling in the sickening crunch that sounded as it met its demise.

"There's one pest that's out of my life forever," she said, grabbing a paper towel to wipe its remains from her salvation.

She grabbed a plastic tumbler and filled it to the top before collapsing in the purple velvet chaise that was her prized possession.

Gazing out at the gently waving branches of the oak tree that graced her front window, she tried to relax.

It was no good. As soon as she let her guard down memories started to invade. And they weren't all bad. For a long while Pence had been everything she'd needed.

She remembered how patient he'd been when critiquing her first efforts at advertising copy. He'd never laughed or shown disdain, no matter how awkward the headline or script construction.

And how he'd loved to surprise her. A midweek picnic aboard a chartered sailboat here. Front row seats to the summer's hottest concert there. A private dinner prepared by the city's top chef whenever anything was seriously amiss.

All wrapped in miles and miles of seemingly sincere promises. He'd painted beautiful pictures of the life they would create together—working opposite each other all day, then playing together all night, making sweet love whenever the mood struck them. He'd even included children in their mythical future: a girl with her hair and his height, and a boy with her eyes and his strength.

She'd thought she'd been transported from her dreary hand-to-mouth existence straight into a fairytale. Unfortunately her happily-ever-after had never put in an appearance.

At least not with Pence. And not in Detroit.

But she'd spent the last five years here in New York, creating a new direction for her story. And, unless she was sadly mistaken, she was almost to the good part.

She put the tumbler of wine to her lips, only to find it empty.

It was time for bed.

She shuffled into the closet that served as her bedroom and crawled beneath the sky-blue goose down duvet that was her biggest extravagance. Her bed was her sanctuary, and normally her lavender-scented sheets relaxed her within minutes.

Not tonight.

Tonight she could only toss and turn, searching for a comfortable place to lay her head.

She was tormented by images of the flowered treasure box that lay hidden under her bed. The one that contained memories she couldn't stand to destroy—and that destroyed her to remember.

Sighing, she twisted the knob on the delicate crystal lamp on her nightstand and clambered out of bed.

With the box settled in her lap, she gently lifted the cover.

Resting there was a picture of her, snuggled against Pence's broad chest at sunset aboard a sailboat. The camera had caught him midlaugh, his blue eyes crinkling, looking happy and relaxed. She could remember the exact moment. She'd felt so safe. So loved. So incredibly sure she was right where she belonged.

The ruby promise ring he'd given her was also there, nestled in its green velvet box. As was the long gold chain he'd insisted she hang it on, so she could wear it "next to her heart." She'd loved to feel it hanging between her breasts, imagining it was him touching her every time the ring had brushed a sensitive area.

There were other pictures, including one taken at the dinner held in honor of her first award-win. He was scowling darkly at the camera, unhappiness obvious in every line of his body.

That was when things had started to go wrong. He hadn't liked it when she'd started succeeding on her own.

At the bottom of the box was the memory she was most dreading. A grainy black-and-white photo of the peanut-size blob that had been her baby at eight weeks.

The baby she had aborted a week later.

She remembered the day the picture had been taken as if it was yesterday. She'd known she was pregnant for three weeks. After the first test had come out positive she'd bought an economy-size pack of pregnancy test strips and taken a new one every morning. The little pink line indicating the baby's existence had got darker and thicker with each passing day, but it hadn't been until her doctor had shown her the blurry black-and-white ultrasound image on a video monitor that she'd allowed herself to believe it was real.

And when he'd found the heartbeat her soul had melted, reforming itself around the tiny little being growing inside her. She'd promised the little peanut that she'd take care of it. That she'd be the best mom ever.

What a joke *that* had turned out to be.

The next night she shaved every last hair from her body and perfumed every crevice before sliding into the sexy white lace lingerie Pence loved. She'd donned silky back-seamed thigh-highs and a skintight black dress that showcased her newly voluptuous breasts.

Her one and only pair of Manolos had been the finishing touch.

When she'd arrived at the intimate French restaurant where she'd arranged to meet Pence she'd known by the slack-jawed look on the face of every man she'd passed that she'd done well.

But by the time the *maître d'* had shown her to the table and helped her settle into a chair under Pence's watchful gaze, her confidence had already been taking a nosedive. His eyes had scraped over her body, taking in the size of her breasts and the curve of her hips.

"Have you gained weight, Becky?" he'd asked.

"N-no," she'd stuttered. "It's just this dress. It forgives nothing."

"Good. You look great, but you know how important it is to stay thin if you want to make it in advertising."

Becky had nodded. "I know," she'd said quietly.

But inside her mind had been screaming. Pregnant women got fat. Would Pence love her when she was fat? It would only be temporary, but his attention span was notoriously short. By the time this baby was born and her body had returned to normal he might have forgotten all about her.

Then what would she do?

"What's wrong?" Pence had asked, reaching out to stroke her hand. "Did I say something to upset you?"

"No, not at all," she'd said with a small smile. "I've just got a lot on my mind."

"That's right." He'd groaned. "You wanted to 'talk.' What is it this time? Is your mom after you to get married again?"

She shook her head. "No, not so far this month," she'd said.

Just then their server had arrived, giving Becky a reprieve. He'd offered Pence a sample from a bottle of freshly uncorked Syrah. Pence had inhaled deeply, then swished the purple liquid around in his mouth. After a long moment he'd given a sharp nod. The waiter had smiled and filled their glasses before fading away.

Pence had looked at her over the rim of his glass. "So what is it?"

Becky had taken a deep breath and reached into her black sequined bag with a trembling hand. "I have a surprise for you," she'd said.

He looked at her suspiciously. "I don't like surprises," he'd said.

She'd pulled out the small silver-wrapped package she'd stowed in her purse and handed it to him.

"I think you'll like this one."

Lord knew he'd talked about his longing for children often enough.

"Humph," he'd muttered as he undid the bow. "We'll see about that."

He'd torn off the wrapping paper in one fell swoop. Becky had felt her heart rise into her throat as he lifted the lid of the box, unsure of what his reaction would be. He'd frowned when he saw the framed picture inside.

"What is this?" he'd demanded.

"It's a picture," she'd said. "An ultrasound."

"An ultrasound? What? Do you have a tumor?"

"N-no," she'd stuttered, taking a deep breath. "I'm pregnant. That's a picture of a baby. *Our* baby."

Pence fell back in his chair. "Pregnant? But how could that be? We take precautions."

Becky had shrugged her shoulders, knowing full well that she wasn't as religious about taking her birth control pills as he supposed she was.

"Apparently not enough," she'd said.

"So this is real? You're not joking?"

"No," she'd whispered. "I'm not."

"But this can't be. You *can't* be pregnant. I have a *wife!*"

Her heart had plummeted, smashing into the polished cement floor at their feet. "You're *married?*" she'd whispered.

"Of course I'm married. I thought you knew that? Didn't you ever wonder why I never spend the night? Or why I never invite you to my house?"

"N-no. I just thought… Well, I didn't think. You said you loved me! You talked about getting married!"

He'd taken her hand again, stroking it gently. "I do love you. And I would love to marry you. But I can't divorce my wife. Her father owns the agency. If I left her I'd lose everything."

"But what about our baby?"

"There can't *be* a baby. Don't you see? You have to get rid of it. It's the only way."

"Get rid of it?"

"Yes. Have an abortion."

"But I don't want an abortion," she'd said. "I want to keep it."

"Then you're on your own," he'd said. "I won't have anything to do with it. If you don't take care of this problem we're done."

"But you just said you love me," she'd whispered.

"Love has nothing to do with it. This is business. And I can't let a little accident like this jeopardize my position with the agency," Pence had said. "Please, just think about it?"

At a loss for words, she'd nodded.

"Good," Pence had said. "Now, if you'll excuse me, I have to attend a dinner party. With my wife."

And with that he was gone.

Becky had stared after him, mouth agape. What was she supposed to do now?

The next week had been a nightmare. She'd crunched numbers, searched the internet and racked her brain, trying to find a way through the predicament she had suddenly found herself in.

Eventually, though, she'd admitted the truth to herself.

She was twenty-three. She had seventy-five thousand dollars in student loans and only made twenty-four thousand dollars a year. There was no way she could raise this baby on her own. And there'd be no help coming from the man she had thought loved her.

Worse, if she kept the baby her career would take a nosedive just when it was starting to get off the ground. The financially secure future she had imagined would disappear in a puff of smoke.

She'd end up like her parents, working two jobs and worrying over every penny she spent for the rest of her life. That was no way to live—or to raise a child.

There was only one choice she could make.

When she'd arrived for her appointment at the family planning clinic it was with cold anger and hot despair stomping on her heart. Rubbing her still-flat belly, she'd made her soon-to-be-aborted baby a promise.

She would never forget him—for it had become a him in her mind—and Pence would pay dearly for this betrayal if it was the last thing she did.

Hot tears leaked down her face now, as she stroked the image. She'd never forgive herself for not standing up to him. For allowing him to control her and for letting him convince her to do something that had felt so wrong.

No man would ever have that much power over her again.

Wiping her tears away with her sleeve, Becky slid the box back under the bed. She had to get to sleep. She had a competition to win—and a living nightmare to defeat.

CHAPTER FOUR

MARK ARRIVED AT the office bright and early, doughnuts and coffee in hand. After the relaxed evening they'd shared he was looking forward to working with Becky today.

Tucking the breakfast items under his chin, he opened his office door, expecting to see it empty. But Becky was already there, pounding away at her computer, punishing the keys with every clack.

"Good morning, early bird! I brought breakfast."

Becky looked up. If the dark circles under her eyes were any indication, Mark thought, she'd never left the office.

She smiled frostily. "Nice of you to make an appearance. Considering how much work we have to do, I thought it would be best to get an early start."

Whoa. Okay. Apparently they were playing a new game.

"Sorry. I thought eight-thirty on a Saturday was plenty early."

"And that's why I'm going to win and you're not," she snapped. "This job takes dedication."

"I've got news for you, princess. Neither one of us is going to win if we can't find a way to merge these two campaigns."

She waved dismissively at him.

"I'm working on it. Why don't you go over there and look for some pretty pictures or something?"

All right. Enough was enough.

"I'll tell you what I'm going to do. I'm going to go over there and come up with another, even more kick-ass idea.

And when David asks what your contribution was I'll tell him you didn't make one. How's that sound?"

She rolled her eyes. "Whatever. Just be quiet about it."

Mark stomped over to his desk and slammed the coffee down. Forget quiet. He was going to work the way he always did. With music blaring.

Seconds later, the discordant sounds of a heavy metal guitar filled the room.

She glared at him, then reached into her drawer and pulled out a pair of headphones.

He loaded up his photo editing program to look at the images he'd already created, but the glare from the overhead lights was killing him. He got up and flipped the lights off. He'd hardly even sat down before she was turning them back on.

"Do you mind?" he said. "I can't work with all that glare."

"Well, I can't write if I can't see the keys," she said,

"Come sit by the window," he said.

"Go work in a cave," she retorted.

He sighed. "Fine. Have it your way. It's not worth fighting about."

She huffed and put her headphones back on.

Mark turned to his computer to get started, but his mind refused to cooperate.

Maybe looking at the existing boards would help. He grabbed the pile from where it lay by the office door and spread the boards out on the plush red carpet, laying the two campaigns side by side.

Then he began to pace back and forth down the line, looking for common ground.

They both featured strong women. And used humor. Maybe...

Becky sighed angrily. "Really? Are you going to pace all day? Because it's really distracting."

He turned to look at her. She was standing with her

hands on her hips, completely unaware of how ridiculously her angry expression contrasted with the giant happy face emblazoned on her oversize T-shirt.

Unbidden, the image of her standing in exactly that position, laughing and naked except for a pair of cheetah-print heels, rose to the front of his brain. How could that free spirit belong to this completely aggravating woman? There had to be a way to get past her anger.

Suddenly he had an idea. Grabbing his jacket, he turned to leave.

"Where are you going?" she asked.

"Out," he said. "See you later."

"But what about—?"

"We can't work together like this. So I'm leaving," he said, shutting the door before she could see the smile on his face.

That would give her something to stew about.

Becky stared openmouthed at the shut door.

Her so-called partner had bailed on her. *Now* what was she supposed to do? True, she hadn't exactly been welcoming, but that didn't give him the right to just quit.

Of course if he didn't come back the promotion would be hers by default. At least it would if she could find the brilliant idea that would allow her to win the competition.

And she *had* to win this. She didn't even care about the promotion so much anymore. She just wanted to kick Pence's pompous ass.

Sighing, she collapsed into her chair and put her head in her hands.

If only Mark wasn't so damn hot. Just being in the same room with him made her think inappropriate thoughts. Thoughts of unbuttoning the faded blue shirt he'd been wearing and licking his chest. Of sliding her hand down the front of his jeans. Of letting him roll down her leggings and take her—right on top of the desk.

She was sorely tempted to do just that. To scratch the itch and move on. After all, she was an empowered, independent woman. Why shouldn't she take what she wanted when he obviously wanted it, too?

Because once would never be enough, that was why. And she knew better than to get involved with a coworker—even a temporary one—ever again.

If sex was out, there was only one thing to do. Work.

An hour later she was still typing indecipherable garbage when the door opened. Mark walked in, carrying a giant F.A.O. Schwartz bag. Trying hard not to feel relieved, she looked at him with a raised eyebrow.

"You went to the toy store?"

"Yep."

He waltzed over to his desk and turned his back on her. She heard a great deal of rustling, then boxes being ripped. Unable to hide her curiosity, she walked up behind him and stood on her tiptoes, trying to see what he was working on.

He turned and she quickly stepped back, nearly falling in the process.

When she caught her balance she saw that he was holding two...*plastic swords?*

Mark looked at her, a serious expression on his face.

"I would like to challenge you to a duel," he said.

"A what?"

"A duel. To settle the problems we seem to be having this morning. If I win you have to give up the attitude. If you win I'll...well, I'll do whatever you want. Leave. Stay. Draw pictures of monkeys. Whatever."

Becky wanted to laugh, but he didn't seem to think what he was proposing was funny.

"Are you serious?"

"As a heart attack."

She licked her lips. "All right."

"Good," he said, a smile quirking at the corners of his mouth. "Do you want to be red or blue?"

"Um…red."

She reached out to take it. "This is actually kind of cool," she said, taking a few test swings.

He nodded, and brought his sword up into fighting position.

"Ready?"

"Sure," she said, imitating his stance.

He started to advance and they circled each other warily.

Suddenly he struck, aiming for her stomach. She moved her sword into position just in time, batting his out of the way before striking back.

He parried her blow and the fight was on. Soon they were whirling around the room, their swords crashing and crackling. Mark kept his expression serious, but Becky felt herself grinning.

She couldn't remember the last time she'd had this much fun with a guy. Or at all.

Mark lunged forward and she backpedaled before stepping on something sharp and cold. The award she'd thrown last night. She cursed at the sudden pain, then grabbed Mark's arm to try and keep herself from falling. Instead she overbalanced, and they fell into a heap, Mark's big body pinning hers to the ground. He pulled one arm free and lightly tapped her forehead with his saber.

"You're dead," he said.

Becky gave in to the laughter frothing in her throat.

"I guess you won, fair and square," she said between giggles.

He grinned down at her.

"Yep. No more attitude from *you,* Sir knight."

"I don't think I could frown if I tried right now," she said.

"Good. I like you better when you're laughing." His

dark eyes took on a liquid sheen. "In fact, there's only one expression I'd rather see," he said.

And without warning he took her lips with his.

His lips crushed down on hers with an urgent demand that she give in to the heat that had been building between them—not just today, but every day since she'd returned from Vegas. And, God help her, but she couldn't ignore it. Couldn't say no.

She let her mouth fall open in silent surrender, giving in to the hunger his searing kisses awakened in her. His tongue plundered her mouth, claiming every inch of it for his own.

She twined her hands in his dark hair and pulled him closer, wanting all that he had to give. She gave up on thought, letting instinct drive her as she arched her body upward, wanting still more.

He took that as the invitation it was, sliding one hand down her body to cup her through her panties.

"Mmm..." he rumbled. "You're already hot for me."

Becky heard herself moan as he slid his hand back up, leaving the sensitive nub of nerves that she wanted him to touch so badly. She grabbed it and put it back, whimpering.

"Wait. Not yet," he said. "I want you naked first."

"Then help me get my clothes off," she growled, starting to squirm out of her shirt.

He pulled it quickly over her head, then whipped her leggings off.

"Yours, too," she said, and within seconds his clothes had joined hers on the floor.

Clothes gone, he lowered himself on top of her and kissed her lips again. She let him in, losing herself in the feel of the intoxicating hardness of his body. She pressed upward, moving her hips against his, almost delirious in her need to connect with him in the most primal way.

"Mark, *now,*" she begged. "I need..."

"Hold on, baby," he said. "I want to taste you first."

In seconds his mouth was on her, licking and nipping at her most sensitive parts.

"Damn, Becky, you have no idea how long I've been wanting to do this," he growled, from somewhere at her center.

She wanted to ask him how long, but the ability to form words left her as he began to suck. She could think of nothing other than the waves of pleasure he was creating. At that moment she would have given anything to keep him right where he was for as long as possible.

Seconds later she peaked, crashing into an abyss of pure sensation.

Mark kissed her as she came down, his mouth even more urgent than it had been before. Knowing what he needed, what they both needed, she wrapped her legs around his waist.

"Mark…now," she whimpered against his mouth.

"Yes, *now,*" he said, and sheathed himself inside her with a quick flex of his hips.

She groaned and clenched her body around him, wanting to keep him there forever.

She let her eyes drift closed as he started moving, losing herself in the sensation.

"No, don't," he whispered. "I want you to look at me."

When she opened them he was looking at her fiercely.

"I want you to see. To know it's me that's doing this to you," he said as he thrusted, pressing against all the right spots.

"Only you," she gasped as he moved inside her. "You're the only one that's ever done this to me."

"God, Becky," he rumbled, heat flooding his gaze as his pace quickened. "You're amazing. Where have you been all my life?"

"I'm. Right. Here. Now," she said.

The heat stabbing through her from his thrusts and the

weight of his gaze melded together into a hot haze of perfection, and she felt her world beginning to splinter.

"Mark, I'm going to..."

"Come for me, Gorgeous Girl," he said, smiling down at her.

And she did, waves and waves of sensation swamping her psyche and blurring his face in front of her.

His expression turned fierce and with a guttural moan he followed her over the cliff.

Afterward they lay twined together, their hearts beating in time. Becky lost herself in the perfection of the moment, unwilling to move and let the real world in again. If she knew the sex would always be like that she'd never let this man go...

When she could put words together again, she said, "You know, until very recently I thought I was bad at that."

"Why on earth would you think that?" Mark said, genuinely shocked. "Becky, you're amazing."

He watched as she flushed, the rosiness reaching all the way down her chest.

"Oh, I...uh...shouldn't have said that out loud. My internal filter must be busted."

He pulled her into his arms. "But you did. Must've been on your mind. Why?" He was surprised at how much he wanted to know.

She looked down at her hands and picked at her fingernails. "Oh, you know. Heard from an ex. Stirred up bad memories."

Judging by the way she was closing in on herself, they must have been spectacularly awful memories. Then he remembered a snippet from the night he'd found her asleep in the kitchen.

"This wouldn't have anything to do with that Pence guy, would it?"

She looked at him sharply. "How would you know that?"

"You were talking in your sleep. That night in the kitchen."

Realization dawned on her face. "Oh. Right. Well, yeah, that's the one. But you know… Every girl's got one."

"Got one what?"

"A voice. One that points out her flaws and harps on her inadequacies. Mine sounds like him."

Mark felt a wave of anger roll across his brain. "If I ever meet this guy I'm going to have a thing or two to say to him. He sounds like a piece of work."

Becky looked at him, a wry smile on her lips.

"Well, you might get your chance."

"Chance to what?"

"Talk to Pence." Her lips twisted, the smile turning into an unconscious snarl. "His agency is pitching to Eden, too."

Mark sat up straighter, surprised.

"How long have you known?"

"Oh…" Becky said, looking up at the clock. "About fifteen hours or so. He emailed last night."

Suddenly her earlier behavior made a lot more sense. Wishing he could save her from her obvious pain, he pulled her close and kissed the top of her head.

"We'll beat him, you know," he said. "Together. That jerk doesn't stand a chance against us."

She murmured her assent, but when he looked at her he could tell her brain was busily working on another problem. Pulling her shirt over her head, she paced over to the whiteboard on the wall.

"We've been going about this all wrong," she said. "Women aren't going to buy our yogurt just because we recognize their awesomeness. That doesn't do anything for them. They're going to buy it if it solves a problem for them. So if the problem is insecurity, we need to position ourselves as a solution."

He watched as she scratched silently on the board with a red marker. Her butt jiggled ever so slightly with the movement, and he found himself wanting to feel the weight of it in his palms again.

She turned to look at him, triumph lighting her eyes.

"I've got it. Check this out. It could be something like, 'Working mom guilt weighing you down? Take an Eden moment and believe.'"

Mark's brain kicked into gear. "Maybe. Or what about, 'Eden. Your shortcut to a more perfect you.'"

Becky wrote it down.

"Good thought. But what about…?"

And they were off and running.

The next time Mark looked up, the sun was setting.

"Wow. We've been at this all day," he said. "You hungry?"

Her stomach growled loudly in response. Laughing, she said, "I guess so!"

"How about I take you out somewhere? My treat."

"I don't think so," she said, crossing her arms over her chest. "I've got laundry and stuff to do tonight."

"Oh, come on. Laundry on a Saturday night? You're not fifty. I'll take you back to my place for dessert," he said, winking suggestively.

She smiled sadly. "Mark, what happened before…it can't happen again. The situation's too complicated. Besides, I don't date people—"

"You don't date people you work with. I know. You keep saying that. But who said anything about dating?"

She flushed. "I don't do what we did this afternoon with coworkers either."

"We were enjoying each other. There's nothing wrong with that."

"You say that now. But if we keep it up before long there will be feelings, then hurt feelings, and eventually heartbreak. I don't do heartbreak," she answered.

Mark felt himself getting frustrated. "You don't do heartbreak. I don't do relationships. So we should be well matched."

"I don't think so..." she said, looking everywhere except at him.

Mark gently turned her to face him.

"Listen to me. This situation *is* complicated. We don't need to add sexual frustration to the mix. After all, we didn't get anywhere today until after we let that go. Right?"

She gave a slight nod.

"And you have to agree the sex is amazing. Probably some of the best I've ever had."

She looked up sharply. "Really?" she said.

"Really."

"I thought it was just... I mean you've been with so many... And I...um...haven't..."

"Becky?"

"What?"

"You're amazing. Period."

She smiled, her cheeks flushing pink. "Thank you."

"You're welcome. So let's just agree to enjoy each other until this—whatever this is—is over and decided. Then we'll go our separate ways. No harm, no foul."

She looked at him. "Do you really think it can be that easy?"

"I know it can," he said. "I won't let it be any other way."

She stared at him for a long moment, an unreadable expression on her face. "I'll think about it," she said.

He nodded, knowing that was probably the best answer he could hope for at the moment.

"Don't think too long," he growled.

She just smiled in response, blowing him a kiss as she walked out through the door.

He knew she'd eventually agree to his proposition. The chemistry they had was too incredible for either of them to walk away. And as long as they kept it to the physical realm no one would get hurt.

Heck, he didn't have enough cash to make her want anything more permanent anyway. She might not *seem* interested in his wallet, but he knew from experience that even the sweetest girls were ultimately moved by money.

For the first time he found himself wishing they weren't.

CHAPTER FIVE

"THIS IS GOOD. Really good," David said after Becky and Mark had pitched their concept to him. "Which one of you came up with it?"

Nice try, Becky thought. She wasn't going to let him knock one of them out of the competition that easily.

"It was pretty organic," she said out loud. "I couldn't tell you which one of us nailed the final line. Could you, Mark?"

"No, not really," he said. "We make a surprisingly great team."

"Good, good—glad to hear it," David said, leaning back in his chair, hands behind his head. "Now we just have to decide how to proceed."

"When is the presentation?" Becky asked.

"October thirtieth at ten a.m."

"Oh. Good. We've got some time, then," she said. More than three weeks, as a matter of fact.

She looked at Mark. He looked back at her, his face pinched with uncertainty. Okay, since he didn't seem to be willing to take charge they were going to do things her way.

"Here's what I think," she said. "I think we need to overwhelm the client with our awesomeness. We need to go in there with print, digital, TV—the works. Obviously we're going to need everybody's help. Mark and I will act as creative leads and work on the big concept stuff—I'm thinking we should tackle TV first—and we'll break everybody else into small teams to handle individual projects. We'll meet with the teams daily, to check their progress and keep everyone on task. When we're satisfied with a project, we'll bring it to you for final approval. Sound good?"

David leaned forward, reluctant admiration showing in every line of his face. "That's a good plan," he said. "If I didn't know better I'd think you'd been handling assignments like this for years."

Don't blush, she told herself. *Don't you dare blush.*

"Thank you," she said. "I've been waiting a long time for an opportunity like this."

"Better get to it," David said. "You have a lot to accomplish in a very short amount of time."

Becky nodded at Mark and they rose, walking silently across the office.

"Good luck," David called as they closed the door. "I'll be watching you. Remember, this is still a competition!"

It was well after eight p.m. before Becky was finally able to sit down at her desk.

It had been a long day of kick-off meetings and strategy sessions, but the teams now had their marching orders and were ready to move forward.

Groaning, she kicked off the patent leather heels that had been torturing her feet all day and massaged her toes. If this was what her life was going to be like from now on she was going to have to invest in some more practical shoes.

And some protein bars, if the tormented sounds issuing from her empty stomach were any indication.

She was seriously considering eating the wizened apple she'd found at the back of a drawer when Mark walked in, carrying a delicious-smelling pizza.

"Dinner is served, my lady," he said, presenting it to her with a flourish.

Becky tore open the box and grabbed a slice of the pepperoni-studded goodness. "It's official," she said, practically moaning as the heavenly mixture of cheese, tomato sauce and bread hit her tastebuds. "You are my hero."

"I try," he said, snagging a piece for himself. "Some days it's easier than others."

They chewed in companionable silence.

"What do you think?" he eventually said. "Can we pull this off?"

"'This' meaning...?"

"The pitch. Three weeks isn't a lot of time to finish everything you proposed."

"Oh. Well, yeah, of course we can. Especially since we've got an entire department of talented people at our disposal."

"That does help," he said between bites. "I've never experienced this level of support before. I'm usually the guy they bring in to salvage a project that's gone off the rails or save an account that's in danger. No one ever really *wants* to work with me."

She thought that sounded kind of lonely, but didn't think he'd appreciate it if she told him so. "It is a pretty unique thing you do. How on earth did you end up being a modern-day dragon slayer?"

"I'm not sure. Just luck, I guess."

"That's some luck you have. You've worked with some of the best agencies out there," she said, eyebrows raised.

"Yeah, well, I've got some connections. It's all about who you know in this business," he said, looking off into the distance.

The sour look on his face was one she'd seen only once before.

"Let me guess. The stepdad?"

"The one and only." Mark grimaced. "He'd do just about anything to keep me out of his house and away from his wife."

"What does he do, anyway?" For some reason, Becky

imagined Mark's stepdad as being some kind of modern-day nobility, living off his inheritance and not doing much of anything.

"You've heard of Kipper, Vonner and Schmidt?"

She snorted. "Of course. They're only the largest ad agency in New York."

"My stepdad's the Kipper. And he bought out Vonner."

"Oh," Becky said, trying not to be impressed. "I guess he *would* have connections."

"Yep. He's the only reason I ever got any work. At least to begin with."

Becky was willing to bet there was more to the story than that. But she wasn't in the mood to push.

"Well, connections or no, you're really good at what you do—at least according to the internet. You've got almost as many awards as I do."

"Ah, so you cared enough to look me up, huh?

"Of course. You didn't think I'd let you back into my pants without making sure you weren't a serial killer first, did you?"

"I wasn't aware that you'd put much thought into the situation at all."

She lowered her eyes, suddenly unable to meet his penetrating gaze. "Well, I may have done it post-pants-getting-into. Last night."

"I see. And what did you decide?"

She smiled. "Well, it was quite a debate. On the one hand, you're great for stress relief."

"Sure—I'll buy that."

"But you're bad for the rep. I had an ice-queen thing going, you know."

"Well, it's too late to save her," he teased. "I distinctly remember seeing her melt Saturday afternoon."

"You might be right. But I was a little worried I might lose my competitive advantage by sleeping with you."

"A valid concern."

"But then I realized engaging in pillow talk is a great way to gather intel."

"True enough."

"There's also the brain goo problem."

"Brain goo?"

"Yeah, when I'm around you and start thinking about what we could do to each other my brain turns to goo."

"Oh," he said, looking devilishly pleased. "Well, that's a good problem to have."

"It is. Especially since the best way to fix it is to do the things I'm thinking about."

"Which means…?"

"Which means you should probably stock up on condoms. I have a very good imagination."

He grinned. "I already did."

"Good. Because you know what I'd like to do right now?"

"What?"

"Have sex in an elevator."

"Did you just…? You want to have…?"

"Sex in an elevator. Yes. It was all I could think about on the way down from David's office this morning."

He shot up from his chair, excitement and desire dancing in his eyes. "Let's go, then. I wouldn't want your brain to be clogged with goo any longer than it needs to be."

A short time later, Becky hit the lobby button so their elevator could resume its descent. Her brain was magnificently clear—and her thighs were wonderfully achy.

Elevator sex was much more acrobatic than it looked in the movies. If Mark hadn't been so wonderfully strong it wouldn't have been possible at all.

Becky peeked over at the man in question just in time to see him rubbing his biceps.

"I guess you got your workout for the day, huh?"

He smiled at her ruefully. "I think I did. Totally worth it, though."

Feeling strangely shy now that the deed was over, Becky blushed and looked up at the ceiling to avoid his eyes—only to find herself looking at a different kind of lens.

"Oh, crap," she breathed. "There's a camera up there."

Mark's jaw dropped. "What are you talking about?"

She pointed. "There's a camera. In the ceiling."

"Oh, well…" he said.

"*Oh, well?* I tell you we were just filmed having sex and you say, *Oh, well?*" she squeaked.

"Becky, look at me," Mark said.

Reluctantly, she did. The intensity in his gaze was almost too much to bear.

"I'm not ashamed of what we've done here. If someone wants to watch, let them," he said. "Besides, no one ever looks at those tapes unless there's a robbery or something."

Looking into the bottomless pits that were his eyes as she was, she couldn't doubt his sincerity. He meant what he was saying. Deciding there was nothing she could do about it anyway, Becky nodded.

"I guess you're right," she said, and reached up for one last kiss.

Just then the elevator bell dinged.

"Well, I guess that puts an end to the evening's festivities," Becky said as she pulled away and stepped out through the open doors into the marble lobby.

"It doesn't have to," Mark replied. "You could come home with me."

For a brief moment Becky found herself wondering what it would be like to fall asleep in his arms. Heaven, probably. Better not to think about it.

"Nah, I don't think so," she said, wrapping her arms tightly around herself. "I'll leave you to your dreams.

They're bound to be steamier than anything I can come up with."

Mark let out a bark of laughter as he held the glass door open for her. "This from the woman who just propositioned me with elevator sex? I don't think you give yourself enough credit, my dear."

"Well," she said as she breezed past him, "I guess it's up to you to top my idea, then. Better put your thinking cap on."

Blowing him a kiss, she strode off into the dark night, waiting until he was out of earshot to give in to the hysterical giggles that were bubbling at the back of her throat. Her sex-kitten act was going to need work if they kept this up very long.

Mark collapsed into the black leather massage chair in the creative conference room and closed his eyes, groaning out loud when the vibrating knobs found the tight spot between his shoulder blades.

It had been another long day spent in meetings and reviewing his team's work. He and Becky hadn't even had a chance to think about their own assignments.

This creative directing stuff was hard.

He was just starting to relax, the tension in his back mostly gone, when his phone rang. When he saw who it was he groaned again. His stepfather always had had impeccable timing.

Mentally steeling himself for a lecture, he hit the answer button.

"Hi, Bill."

There was a pause as the man on the other side of the line took a sip from a clinking glass. "Hello, son."

Mark cringed. He hated it when Bill called him that.

"What can I do for you, Bill?"

"Oh, nothing…nothing. Just checking in to see how the Eden thing is going."

"You know about that?"

His stepfather snorted. "Of course. I know everything that's going on in this industry, son. So, have you closed the deal yet?"

Mark sighed. "No, we haven't even gotten to the pitch stage yet. But it's going very well. In fact, I'm acting as creative director on the campaign…"

"That's right. You and that Becky girl. I hear she's pretty hot stuff."

"You have no idea," Mark said.

"Yeah, well, you'll keep your hands to yourself if you know what's good for you," Bill said. "It's never a good idea to mix business with pleasure."

Now it was Mark's turn to snort. "Is that what you told my mom? I seem to remember she worked for you before she married you. Unless that was a business arrangement too…"

"Just keep your hands where they belong and do this right," Bill snapped. "Our family's reputation is on the line here."

"How do you figure? I never tell anyone we're related unless I have to."

"Maybe so. But the ad world is a small place. Those who matter know you're my son."

"Stepson," he snarled. "As you never failed to remind me when I was living under your roof."

"Yes, well, that was then. This is now. There's a place for you at my agency anytime you want it. Especially if you can bring—"

"I assure you, I never will," Mark broke in, and hung up.

He couldn't take any more of his stepfather's asinine advice today. Although he had deflected the question, Mark knew that love had very little to do with Bill's marriage to his mother. She had told him so herself—on their wedding day.

He had found her pinning a flower in her hair in her opulent palace of a bedroom at Bill's house. She'd looked more beautiful than he'd ever seen her.

She'd seen him in the reflection of her mirror and smiled. "Come here, handsome," she'd said. "Let me look at you."

He'd moved to hug her, then asked the question that had been driving him crazy ever since he'd heard about their engagement.

"Mom? Why are you marrying Bill?"

"Because he asked me to," she'd answered.

"But you don't love him."

"I don't have time to wait for love," she'd said as she straightened the gray-and-white striped tie of his morning suit. "I'm not getting any younger, but you *are* getting older. And more expensive. This way I'll have a partner I can count on—and you'll have a father."

"But I don't want him to be my dad," Mark had said. "He doesn't even like me."

"He does, too. He just doesn't know you very well. Be your usual charming self and everything will be fine," his mother had said.

She couldn't have been more wrong. Bill had never shown him anything other than complete and utter disdain. Mark was sure that his stepfather considered him to be nothing more than an annoyance—a piece of unwanted baggage that unfortunately could not be parted from his wife.

He would have been better off growing up poor and fatherless.

Suddenly a soft hand landed on his shoulder.

"You look lost in thought," Becky said.

Mark shook his head to clear it. "Just relaxing," he said, and pulled her down on his lap.

She put her head on his shoulder and for a moment they just sat together, the vibrations from the still-operating massage chair the only noise.

Then she sighed. "Being a creative director is way less fun than I thought it would be."

He laughed. "You know, I was just thinking that. I haven't done any actual work today, but I'm completely exhausted."

"Me, too," she said. "But I was thinking I should try to write now that it's quiet."

She shifted on his lap, preparing to get up. But when Mark caught a glimpse of a black lace stocking as her skirt crept up her thigh all thoughts of work vanished from his brain.

"What's this?" he said, running his hand up the silken material and under the lace top.

"Oh, you know… Just a little something to keep you wondering," she said, blushing.

"Oh, I'm wondering, all right," Mark growled, mentally picturing her riding him wearing only those stockings. "I'm wondering what else is under that skirt."

She shrugged. "A lady never tells. You'll have to find out for yourself."

That was all the encouragement he needed. He let his hand wander up her smooth thigh, tracing the elastic of the garter up to where it met the satiny belt. Then his hand drifted down, toward the middle, looking for the top of her panties. But nothing blocked his way, and soon he felt the soft roundness of her mound under his fingers.

"You're not wearing any underwear," he said, and a bolt of lightning struck his groin, leaving him rock hard and aching for her.

She put a mocking hand over her mouth, unable to hide her grin. "Oops, I must have forgotten. Silly me."

"You. Are. So. Hot," he said, stroking her bare center and grinning when he saw her expression liquefy.

He plunged one finger slowly into her core, enjoying teasing her. But it wasn't enough. He knew he had to have her.

He drew his finger out and nipped her ear. "Stand up for me, Gorgeous Girl."

She did, her legs shaking the tiniest of bits.

"I'm standing," she said, her voice husky with desire. "Now what?"

Mark remembered where they were and paused. "Hang on just a second," he said, and pushed a chair under the door handle. It wouldn't do to have one of the cleaning people walk in on them.

Crossing the floor in two strides, he returned to where Becky was standing, looking beautiful and unsure. "Now, where were we?" he growled.

She smiled. "I think you were trying to get a better look at my stockings."

"Oh, yeah." He grinned. Reaching behind her, he pulled her zipper down and her gray wool skirt fell to the floor, leaving her wearing only the stockings and heels on her bottom half. He paused, taking a moment to appreciate the perfection of her body. Overcome with a fierce sort of want he couldn't remember ever feeling before, he pulled her toward him.

"I want you right here, right now," he said, sitting down again.

"In the chair?"

"You better believe it," he said, freeing himself from his pants and boxers as quickly as he could. "Get over here."

Smiling, she straddled him, plunging on top of him the second he had a condom on. They both groaned, and Mark grabbed her hips, helping her to find her rhythm. He'd never met a woman who fit him so perfectly. So deliciously. If only relationships depended solely on sexual compatibility…

In no time at all she was arching backward, pushing her breasts into his face as she rocked. He kissed the tender swell of them, feeling grateful that such an amazing woman was giving herself to him.

To show her exactly how grateful he was, he slipped a finger into the place where their bodies met, searching for the nub that brought her so much pleasure.

"Oh, God, I think I'm—"

The last bit of her sentence became a wordless yell as she spasmed over him. Seconds later, he allowed himself to follow her over the edge.

She collapsed on top of him and they sat quietly, catching their breath. Just then, his stepfather's unwanted voice echoed in his head. *Keep your hands to yourself if you know what's good for you.*

Clearly the man had no idea what he was talking about. Nothing could be better for him than this. If there was a more satisfying way to relieve stress he'd yet to find it.

Kissing her neck, he said, "I want to do that again."

"Already?" She laughed. "Give a girl a moment to recover."

"Not here. I want to take you home and love you properly."

She bit her lip, clearly trying to think of an excuse not to go.

Taking her head in his hands, he looked deep into her eyes. "Don't overthink it. I just want to spread you out on a bed and do you right. Just this once."

"All right. But just this once."

CHAPTER SIX

BECKY COLLAPSED ONTO a fluffy white pillow, letting out a deep breath as her heart rate returned to normal.

"I've said it before, and I'm sure I'll say it again, but you really are Magic Man," she said. "I can't remember the last time I felt this relaxed."

Mark raised himself up on one elbow and grinned. "Glad to be of service," he said. "Think I should go into business?"

Becky giggled. "Sure—I can picture the ad now. It could read something like, 'Forget the massage. Spend an hour with the Magic Man.' And there'd be a picture of you, wearing nothing but a top hat and holding a wand."

He groaned. "Don't quit your day job, babe."

At the mention of work Becky felt some of the tension return. "Day job? Try twenty-four-seven job. I never stop thinking about the pitch. Do you?"

"Only when I'm otherwise occupied by you," Mark said, eyes smiling. "Hey, think we could work orgasmic sex into the Eden campaign?"

Becky laughed as her stomach growled. "I don't know. I'm too hungry to think. But maybe if you feed me I'll think of a way."

Pulling on his boxers, Mark said, "Message received. Let me see what I can rustle up."

As he padded the short distance over the hardwood floor to the kitchen area Becky couldn't help but admire the gorgeous contours of his muscled body. He was by far the best-looking man she'd ever slept with—not that there'd been that many.

She hadn't had time for boys in high school, and had spent her undergrad years being too afraid of making the same mistake her mother had—dropping out of college to get married—to allow herself to have any real relationships.

In fact, other than a few drunken encounters, there hadn't been anyone until Pence. And there certainly hadn't been anyone after him.

She sighed. What a waste of a decade. If Mark had taught her anything, it was that sex could be lots of fun—especially when there were no strings attached.

Mark's voice brought her out of her reverie. "What do you want? Chinese, Thai, or pizza?"

She blinked. "You have enough stuff in that tiny refrigerator to make all of that?" It didn't look big enough to house much more than a six-pack of beer.

"Nope. I've got exactly five green olives, two hunks of moldy cheese, and one gallon of expired milk. We're getting takeout."

"Oh. Thai, I guess," she answered, leaving her cozy nest on the futon to peek at the menus he was holding out. He pulled her against his chest so they could look at the menus together, but all she could think about was the delicious way he smelled: a little bit spicy, a little bit outdoorsy, and all male.

Suddenly an idea struck her. "Maybe we could work orgasms into the campaign," she said.

"What?"

"Orgasms. Eden. I bet we could do some funny videos linking them."

He blinked. "I thought you had to eat before you could have any more brilliant ideas?"

"Yeah, well, get me some of that pineapple curry and I'll be even more brilliant," she answered.

"Coming right up," he said, and punched the number into his phone.

* * *

A couple of hours later the block of granite that did double duty as a table and a kitchen counter was littered with take-out boxes and crumpled sheets of paper.

Becky yawned and stretched. "I think we've got some pretty solid scripts here, don't you?"

"I think we've got some award-winners here—that's what I think," Mark said.

"Me, too," she said, yawning again. "Which is good, because it's definitely time for me to go home."

Mark glanced up at the clock on the microwave. "It's practically morning already. Why don't you just stay?"

A small ping of alarm sounded in her brain. Coming over for a quick hookup was one thing. Staying overnight was definitely relationship territory.

"Two o'clock is hardly morning," she said. "Besides, we've got work tomorrow. I'd rather not be seen wearing the same clothes two days in a row."

"Nobody will notice," he said, his voice softly cajoling.

"No? Not any of the fifty bazillion people I have meetings with tomorrow? I think they will."

"Well, you could always stop at home in the morning. Before going to work."

"I've got an eight a.m. meeting. No time." It was just supposed to be a quick gab with Jessie at the diner. But she'd put it on her calendar, so it counted.

Mark looked at her for a long moment. She wasn't sure what he saw, but finally he sighed and looked away.

"Fine. I'll call you a cab."

"I can walk."

"No. You can't. Not at this hour."

"Really. I can!"

"Just let me do it, okay? I'll worry about you otherwise."

She shut her mouth with a snap, unsure of what to say.

No one had worried about her in a long time. It felt good to know that he cared.

But he wasn't supposed to care. And neither was she. Caring led to relationships, which led to heartbreak—and she was sure as hell never going through that again.

"Okay," she mumbled. "Call me a cab. I'll go get dressed."

Becky poured milk into her coffee and watched the cheerful chaos that was morning in the diner, waiting for Jessie to digest what she'd told her.

"So you went to his place? Big deal," Jessie said, leaning back against the red vinyl booth.

"I thought you said that was out of bounds in office affairs?" she answered.

Jessie shrugged. "I just said that to make you feel better. Think about it: most people have to have sex in their homes. We don't all have a private office to escape to when we decide we're in the mood for a booty call."

"We've only actually done it in our office once…"

Jessie covered her ears. "*Eww.* That's enough. I don't want to know where else you guys have been. I have to work there, too, you know."

"All right, all right, I won't tell you. It's just that, well, it feels safe at work. Once we venture beyond the building it all starts to feel too relationshippy," Becky said.

Just then Rachel, their favorite waitress, arrived and slammed down their pancakes. "Here you go, ladies! Two pancake short stacks, just like usual. Enjoy!"

"Thank you, Rachel," Becky said.

"No problem," the matronly woman said. "Eat up. You're getting too skinny!"

Both women were silent as they buttered the stacks and dived in. After the first bite, Jessie pointed at Becky with her fork.

"You know what your problem is?"

"What?"

"You're overthinking it. This thing with Mark is just like the stack of pancakes in front of you. They're gorgeous to behold, delicious to experience, but when you've had enough you won't be sad, will you?"

Becky shook her head.

"Exactly. You'll enjoy your post-pancake carb coma and forget about them. Until the next time you get a craving."

With that she took another giant bite and grinned. "These are really yummy."

Becky laughed. She had a point.

"I don't think he'd like being compared to pancakes."

Jessie raised an eyebrow. "You don't think he'd like you to eat him up?"

"I don't know. Maybe I'll ask him."

"Good girl. But mind if I give you a tip?"

"What?"

"Don't use maple syrup in bed. Too sticky."

Becky blushed. "I'll try to remember that."

And just like that everything was right in her world again. She wasn't having a relationship. She was just enjoying a good breakfast after a long fast.

That she could deal with.

Mark hovered at the door to their office, afraid to go in. After Becky had left his apartment he'd tossed and turned all night.

It had been a great evening. He'd enjoyed every second of it. The sex, the food, the brainstorming...he'd never experienced anything like it. He certainly hadn't wanted it to end.

But when he'd realized how much it mattered to him that Becky got home safely—and how much he'd rather she didn't leave at all—reality had crashed in. He'd never worried about any of his other bedmates like that. In fact he was usually the one rushing them out through the door.

After Mark had seen her into a cab he'd collapsed into bed, but sleep had been the furthest thing from his mind. All he'd been able to think about was Becky. He could no longer pretend this was a simple office affair. He was starting to have feelings for this woman. Big feelings. And that was no good.

He didn't do relationships. Period. And even if he did want a relationship he couldn't have one with Becky. It was just too complicated.

It had been almost time to go to work when he'd finally faced the truth. As much as he was enjoying their time together, he had to put a stop to it. If he didn't, both he and Becky were going to get hurt.

No matter how cool Becky seemed, he couldn't take a chance on her. Sandra had taught him that love wasn't worth the pain.

Besides, she deserved someone who had enough money to take care of her. Not someone who had voluntarily cut himself off from his rich family's largesse.

Taking a deep breath, he walked through the door. And stopped dead. Becky was sitting cross-legged on the floor in a patch of sunshine, laptop perched precariously on her knees. She was jamming to something on her iPhone, humming tunelessly along to whatever song was piping through her headphones.

She looked relaxed and happy, which was a far cry from the stressed-out ball of nerves he had expected to encounter this morning.

He must have made some kind of noise because she turned. When she saw him she smiled, the grin lighting up her whole face.

It took his breath away. God, she was beautiful.

"Hey, Magic Man," she shouted, clearly not realizing her headphones were in.

He laughed in spite of himself, motioning to her to take them out.

"What?" she yelled. "Oh." Giggling, she removed her headphones. "Oh. That is better," she said, unwinding herself from her spot on the floor. "Okay, let's try this again. Good morning, Magic Man."

He smiled back at her. "Good morning."

She crossed over to him and reached up for a kiss. At the last minute he turned his cheek.

She frowned. "What's with the shy act?"

He shrugged. "I just think we should cool it during office hours."

"You do, huh? That's a first. But whatever…"

She turned and went to her desk, but not before he saw the hurt that flashed across her face.

"I've got our scripts all typed up and polished. If you want, we can go present them to David now."

He took a deep breath, knowing that if he didn't tell her what he had come to say now he never would.

"Good idea. But can we talk for a minute first?"

"Okay," she said. "This sounds serious. What's up?"

"I don't think this is a good idea anymore," he blurted.

"You don't like the campaign?"

"No, I meant this," he said, motioning to the two of them. "Us. I don't think we should pursue a personal relationship anymore."

She blinked slowly. "Wow. Okay, that's a change in tune. May I ask what prompted it?"

He shrugged again. "There's just too much going on right now. We need to focus on the task at hand."

It wasn't a lie. He definitely did need to focus on his career right now. And so did she. The fact that doing so would keep all those pesky feelings at bay was just a fringe benefit.

"I thought we decided that the best way to stay focused was to give in to our personal desires," she said, in the same carefully professional voice he had used.

"I changed my mind," he said.

She shook her head as her face flushed with anger. "You're a piece of work—you know that? First you come on all hot and heavy, begging me to give this a shot, telling me how much fun we'll have, and then, just when I'm starting to enjoy myself, you pull the plug."

"I'm sorry," he said, fighting the urge to grab her in his arms and kiss her until she forgot all about this conversation.

"I should have known better than to trust you to keep your word," she snarled. "You're a selfish bastard, just like every man I've ever known."

Grabbing her computer, she headed for the door.

"Where are you going?"

"To my office. I can't stand to look at you right now."

"This *is* your office."

"Fine. I'm going to Jessie's office, then."

"What about the scripts?"

"I'll email them to you. You can present them to David by yourself."

Then she swept out, slamming the door behind her.

Mark scrubbed his face with his hands, fairly certain he'd made a gigantic mess of things. But at least he'd done it before anyone's heart had gotten involved.

That would have been even worse.

Becky sat nursing a cup of tea in the kitchen, keeping an ear cocked toward the hallway door so she could escape out the back way if necessary. So far she'd managed to avoid Mark for three days, and she had every intention of continuing the trend.

It had been easy enough to do. She'd kept herself busy managing the print and digital teams, and let him take the lead on the broadcast stuff.

It pained her to give up control of her ideas, but the only other option was to sit in a room with him and wonder what she had done to turn him off. And, worse, what it was about her that made men want to run—even when all she wanted was sex.

Her instincts had been right. She was better off without a man in her life, even if the sex was awesome. There were enough adult sites selling sex toys to keep her satisfied for decades—no emotional entanglements required.

The only thing they couldn't do was make her laugh. But as long as Jon Stewart and Stephen Colbert continued to make their nightly TV appearances she'd have plenty of funny men in her life. It would have to be enough.

She was debating whether she should make a second cup of coffee when she heard a familiar roar in the hallway.

"Becky? Becky, where are you?" David shouted. Then, only slightly more quietly, "Just like a woman. Never around when you need her."

She slammed her cup down and strode out into the hallway.

"I'm right here," she said.

He turned, a slippery smile on his face. "Oh, there you are. I've been looking everywhere for you."

"Well, I've been sitting in the kitchen for the last twenty minutes, so…"

"Never mind, never mind—you're here now. Come with me, my dear. We need you in the production studio."

"All right," she said as they hurried down the hallway. "What's going on?"

"It's these videos," he said, holding the door open for her.

"They were brilliant on paper, but they're just not coming together. I want you to have a look."

She stopped just inside the door, waiting for her eyes to adjust to the darkness of the room. When her vision returned she saw Mark frowning into one of the eight monitors, unhappiness etched into every line of his face.

He glanced in their direction, and when he caught sight of her she was pretty sure she saw a relieved expression cross his face.

"Hey," he said.

"Hey, yourself," she said. "What did you do to our videos? I hear they lost their magic."

He ignored the dig.

"I'm not sure. Take a look and tell me what you think."

He hit a button on the keyboard and the videos began to play. Becky tried to pay attention, but found herself getting distracted by the man next to her. She could feel the heat coming from him like a physical thing. It called to her, drawing her in like a moth to a flame.

What *was* it about this man? Why did the very sight of him turn her knees to jelly? It wasn't fair. Especially since he didn't seem to feel the same way.

"So what do you think?" he asked, and she realized the videos had stopped playing.

"I'm not sure. Play them again." This time she would actually watch them.

The problem became apparent almost immediately, but she let the reel play to the end before she gave her opinion.

"It's simple. The actress you hired thinks she's in a porn movie. She doesn't appear to have a funny bone in her body. And those boobs make her look like Jessica Rabbit. The women in these videos are supposed to be way more real and way funnier."

"So what do you think we should do?" Mark asked.

"Start over."

"What?" David yelled. "We can't do that. We've already spent too much. We can't hire another actress."

"We have to," Becky snapped. "These videos are what's going to make people remember Eden. We can run all the polished TV ads we want, but if we don't find a way to connect with people, to entertain them and get them talking—well, Eden's just going to end up being another yogurt in the refrigerator case. And we're going to end up fired."

"But we don't even have the business yet! I can't possibly put up the money to do a whole new shoot—the first one cost almost fifty thousand dollars!"

Mark looked at her, a silent plea in his eyes. She thought about the night they had scripted them. About how excited he'd been. And how badly she wanted to win this account. She made the only decision she could.

"Fine. I'll do it," Becky blurted.

"You'll what?"

"I'll be your actress...but only for the version we show at the pitch. It's either that or we scrap the whole idea. We certainly can't show these to the client."

David and Mark stared at her, plainly flabbergasted.

"Are you sure you want to do that?" Mark asked.

"No, but I will. Just as long as we all understand that if they like them and want to go ahead with the video campaign, we make them give us the budget to shoot them with real actresses—actresses that I choose."

"Do you think you can pull it off?" David asked.

"Oh, I'm fairly certain I can."

"How certain?"

"Very. I can fake an orgasm right now if you want me to prove it."

David blanched. "No! No, that won't be necessary. I trust you. Just get it done. Quickly."

Then he scrabbled backward out through the door as quickly as he could.

Mark looked at her. "I guess it's just you and me, kid."

"Yep. I guess so," she said, trying to ignore the way her pulse was pounding.

"I've missed you."

He'd missed her? He'd *missed* her? How dared he…? It was his fault they'd been apart in the first place.

"Good," she said. No way was she going to admit that she'd missed him, too.

He looked at her, a rueful smile on his face. "I guess I deserved that," he said.

She nodded. "Yep. You did. But never mind that. We've got a video series to film. When do you want to start?"

He sighed. "Well, unfortunately the camera crew we used the first time has moved on to another project, and I'm not sure where to get another one on such short notice."

"Camera crew? Who needs a camera crew? We're both professionals. Let's just do it ourselves."

He raised an eyebrow. "Seriously? You think we can?"

"I don't know if you've seen the agency equipment closet, but we've got some pretty sweet cameras. As long as you can push a button we'll be fine."

"Okay," he said. "You're on. I'll book a room and we can start filming tonight."

Her mind stuttered. "A room?"

"A hotel room, silly. That's how you scripted it, remember?"

Oh. Yeah. She had. But she wasn't sure she felt comfortable being alone in a hotel room with Mark now that their relationship was back to being strictly professional.

Unfortunately she had already volunteered. She couldn't back out now.

"Right," she said. "That makes sense. Okay, you set it up and email me the details. I'll meet you there at seven."

Becky decided to spend the rest of the afternoon getting herself camera-ready. While she'd told David she wanted the videos to look real, she didn't need the client to see her in her current frazzled, haven't-looked-in-a-mirror-in-four-days state.

After three hours at the salon, getting her hair blown out, eyebrows waxed, nails manicured and face professionally made up, she was feeling much better.

Especially since she had every intention of billing it all to the agency. Now all she needed was a few outfit changes and she'd be all set. The scripts she'd written called for both yoga pants and exotic lingerie.

The yoga pants she had. But the other scenes called for a visit to her favorite lingerie boutique. She hoped David had been billing their clients regularly, because this trip was going to cost him.

She wandered around the store, looking at frilly pink confections, slinky red gowns, and black lace fantasies, unable to decide which would be best. Finally she decided to just try them all on.

Once in the fitting room, she was struck by an idea that she knew was both awesome and completely evil. Since she couldn't decide what to buy, she'd snap pics and send them to Mark.

After all, he was the art director. It was only fitting that he be in charge of wardrobe. Before she could talk herself out of it Becky took a picture of herself in a slinky red gown and composed a message to send to Mark.

Can't decide what wardrobe choices to buy for the shoot, she texted. Should I get this one?

After hitting Send, she quickly changed into the next outfit and prepared to repeat the exercise. But before she could even take the picture, her phone pinged with Mark's return text.

Hell, yes.

She grinned and sent the next picture.

How about this?

Please do.

After sending the third picture, she sat back and admired her reflection. The push-up cups in the black lace chemise made her breasts look huge…making her waist look tiny by comparison. Her hair was thicker than she'd ever seen it, and her face practically glowed under the makeup.

She might not be a porn star, but she looked pretty damn good.

Finally, her phone pinged.

GET THEM ALL, his text read.

Her veins buzzed with triumph. Hopefully, he was sincerely regretting his hasty decision to end the physical side of their relationship right now. He certainly would be by the time the night was over if she had anything to say about it.

CHAPTER SEVEN

MARK DRUMMED HIS fingers impatiently on the glass tabletop. Everything was ready for the shoot. Now all he needed was for his talent to show up. Hopefully with her clothes on.

He'd chosen to rent a suite instead of a hotel room. He'd told himself that it was so they'd have plenty of space to set up their equipment, but if he was being honest he knew it was so he'd have somewhere to retreat if the temptation to touch her got to be too much.

Lord knew the pictures she'd sent this afternoon had been enough to get him rock hard. She looked like something out of his fantasies, her innocently mischievous expression contrasting wildly with the siren's body underneath. He was certain better men than him would fall victim to the silent promise in every pixel of those images.

But he wouldn't. Couldn't.

If he touched her again he wouldn't be able to stop. And if he didn't stop touching her, their hearts would get involved. And then, if he wasn't careful, he'd find himself with a life full of... His mind showed him pictures of weddings and babies and laughing families. But he shook his head, rejecting the images.

It would all end in heartbreak. Even if they made it to the altar, love never lasted. She'd get bored, find someone better and wealthier, and he'd end up crushed. It was better not to go there in the first place.

He jumped at the sudden knock on the door.

Becky had arrived. After taking a moment to push all

his inappropriate emotions back into the box where they belonged, Mark opened the door.

And felt lust roaring to life all over again.

Gone was the fresh-faced woman he worked with. In her place was a primped and polished beauty who looked as if she'd just stepped out of a magazine cover.

"Wow," was all he could say.

She raised her eyebrow. "Is that your new version of hello?"

"No. Sorry. Come in. It's just…you look fantastic."

"Well, it's not every day I find myself starring in an advert," she said as she breezed past him. "I thought I should look the part."

Once inside the door, she stopped dead and whistled.

"Whoa! When you do something, you don't believe in going halfway, do you?"

The suite *was* pretty spectacular. Dark mahogany wood covered the floor and supported the sky-high ceiling. The bed was king-size and ultraplush, with what seemed to be a mountain of fluffy blankets and pillows piled on top. Through a door to the right there was a kitchen area that gleamed with stainless steel appliances and sparkling granite counters. At the back, just in front of the two-story-tall windows, was a living area outfitted with a white leather couch and vivid red club chairs. And, although Becky couldn't see it, Mark knew she'd die when she saw the bathroom. It had a tub big enough to swim in, a two-person shower, and more complimentary beauty products than he'd ever seen.

"Well, you know… This is on the company. I figured why settle for anything less than the best?" he said, grinning.

She laughed. "We're on the same wavelength, then. I don't even want to tell you how much I spent in the lingerie store."

A strange kind of hunger growled to life in the pit of his stomach. "Well, if the pictures you sent were any indication, I'd say whatever you spent was well worth the cost."

"Well," she said with a wicked smile, "you'll be seeing them in the flesh in just a few minutes. Where do you think we should start?"

The bed. That was where he wanted to start…and finish. But only if he was in it with her. Unfortunately, that was the one place he couldn't go.

"Maybe we should tackle the 'before' parts of the skits first, then tackle the 'after.' That way you don't have to keep changing back and forth."

Plus, that way, he wouldn't have to see her in that sexy lingerie for a while.

"Okay," she said. "Why don't you get set up? I'll get changed."

He nodded, wondering if he should take a cold shower or slam his hand in a drawer or something while she was gone. He needed to do something drastic or there would be no way to keep his libido under control.

Three hours later they were done with every yoga-panted scenario the scripts called for, plus a few more Mark had thrown in just for good measure. It was time to move on to the sexy stuff.

God help him.

He busied himself setting up lights in the bedroom area, telling himself that it was no big deal. After all, the woman who'd been their lead actress in the first version of these videos had been a bona fide porn star.

He'd made it through *that* shoot with barely more than a tingle in his nether regions. Surely he could do the same now? It might be Becky playing the part, but it was still business. Sex had no place here.

None.

"All right, I'm ready," Becky called from somewhere behind him. "Where do you want me?"

Mark turned, his most professional smile on his face. "Did you remember to bring the yogurt con…?"

The sentence trailed off as his mind registered what Becky was wearing. She looked like sin made flesh. Her blond curls tumbled over shoulders covered only by a pair of spaghetti-thin red satin straps.

His eyes traveled farther down, noticing that the straps led to a slinky red gown that made the most of Becky's perfectly mounded breasts, begging him to touch them. Then it followed the contours of her itty-bitty waist before splitting into a thigh-high slit.

The leg that peeked through was wrapped in a matching red fishnet stocking, and was made to look all the longer by the spiky cheetah-print stilettos.

"Hey, I remember those shoes," he said, cursing himself for his stupidity the moment the words were out of his mouth.

She laughed. "Yeah, I figured I was spending enough of David's money without going shoe shopping, too. And these babies certainly had the desired effect the first time around."

Inwardly he groaned, remembering that first night. He hadn't thought she could possibly look any hotter than she had when he'd met her in Vegas. He'd been wrong.

"You look amazing," he said. There. That was innocent enough. He was just giving the lady her due. She didn't need to know how very close he was to ripping those amazing clothes off her body and throwing her on the bed.

She grinned happily and did a pirouette.

"I know. I really should buy things like this more often. It does wonderful things for a girl's self-confidence."

Then she swished over to the bed, crossing her legs seductively after she dropped onto its surface.

"In answer to your earlier unasked question—yes, I did bring the yogurt container. And now I am prepared to do nasty things with this spoon," she said, holding out her intended weapon.

Mark watched helplessly as she brought it to her lips and licked it seductively, then plunged it deep into her mouth. Throwing her head back, she pulled it slowly out, then traced it down her neck to linger at the top of her breasts.

Mark groaned involuntarily, every muscle in his body aching with the need to kiss her everywhere the spoon had touched—and in many places it hadn't.

Her head popped up and she grinned.

"Guess I'm doing that right, huh?"

"I'd say. You may have missed your calling as a porn star."

Her nose wrinkled. "Nah. Too many scary dudes. But maybe I could moonlight as a pinup girl. At, like, an ice cream parlor or something. Ice cream really does make me hot."

He laughed. It was good to know that the Becky he knew was still in there somewhere.

"All right, let's not get ahead of ourselves," he said. "First we've got to make you a video star."

She nodded. "Okay, let's do it."

"So, in one script you have yourself taking a bite while in bed, then having a screaming orgasm. Want to start there?"

She blushed. "Um…let's start with something tamer, shall we? I think I need to work up to that."

"Okay," he said, flipping through script pages. "Well, that thing you were just doing there was pretty close to what you've got here. But at the end you've got to call to your husband and tell him to—and I quote—'Get in here and take care of business.'"

"Right," she said, a worried look on her face. "That seemed like a much better idea when someone else was doing it, but what the hell? I said I wanted this to seem sexy and real and kind of funny, right? I can do funny sexy stuff. I'm almost sure of it."

"Based on what I just saw, I have absolute faith in you," he said. "Let's give it a try. Ready?"

"Just a minute," she said, and paused to plump her hair and her breasts. "How's my lipstick?"

"It's…fine," he said, although it took everything he had to tear his eyes from her chest.

"Good. Let's do it."

He nodded and began the countdown. "Three, two, one…action!"

At his signal she began her routine with the spoon again. But this time she added in strategic little whimpers and moans.

Mark felt himself growing hotter and harder as the seconds ticked by. Just when he thought he couldn't take it anymore, she sat straight up in bed.

"David!" she shouted. "Turn off the TV and get in here. I need you to take care of some business!"

The last part was said with a comically suggestive waggle of her eyebrows and Mark just barely managed to shut the camera off before giving in to the gut-deep laughter that was begging for release. "Oh. My. God," he said between laughs. "Did you have to use David's name?"

"You're darn right I did," she said. "Revenge is sweet." But she was smiling as she said it, and soon she was laughing, too.

Mark collapsed on the bed next to her and she let herself sag against him, still giggling. They sat like that for what felt like forever. As soon as one stopped laughing, the other would erupt in a contagious peal and they'd both be off again.

At long last the laughing fit ended and they sat, gasping, trying to catch their breath.

Mark looked in her sparkling green eyes and felt something shift way down deep in his stomach. He'd never met a woman he could laugh like that with before.

Refusing to put a name to the emotion that threatened to make itself known, he kissed her forehead. "I really did miss you, Gorgeous Girl. You're one funny lady."

She jerked back, anger suddenly sparking in her eyes. "Well, I'm glad I can make you laugh, if nothing else," she said.

Whoa. He wasn't sure what he had said that was so wrong, but he definitely wished he hadn't said it. Time to get back to business.

"All righty, then. I guess we should move on, huh?"

"Give me just a minute to change into the next outfit," she said, and clacked angrily out of the room.

Mark took a deep breath. One sexy scene down, three to go. It was going to be a hell of a long night.

Becky slathered on one last coat of crimson lipstick. They were down to the last scene. The faked orgasm scene. The one she was least sure she could pull off.

But the rest of the shoot had gone much better than she'd ever dreamed it would, so there was hope. She looked at her artificially rumpled reflection and took a deep breath. So far she'd done well, both in front of the camera and in the psyche of the man who was trying to resist her. Now all she had to do was bring it home.

This black lace get-up could only help.

She stalked out to the bedroom area, trying to remember exactly how the orgasm scene had gone in *When Harry Met Sally.* Surely it couldn't be that hard?

A low whistle brought her back to the present.

"Damn, Becky, what are you trying to do? Kill me?" Mark asked in a strained voice.

Becky raised her eyebrow. "You're the one who decided

you didn't want to touch me anymore," she said. "So, if you die from what you're seeing here tonight, I'm thinking they'd have to rule it a suicide."

He sighed and waved her over to the bed. "*Touché.* Let's just get this over with, okay?"

As Becky crossed to the bed she swished her hips as much as she was able. Then she spread her golden hair out on the pillows and prepared to play her part.

"Ready?" she called to her reluctant cameraman.

He shook his head. "No. You still look too controlled. Let your limbs go a little."

She tried to let her arms and legs relax, but felt strangely tense under Mark's dark-eyed gaze. "How's this?"

He moved forward. "No. That's not how you look when you're…in the moment. May I touch you?"

She could only nod, her mouth suddenly dry.

Gently he cupped her knees, splaying them apart slightly. The fabric of the black lace chemise fell to the side, revealing the matching panties underneath. Mark's eyes flashed, dark with desire.

"There. That's better. Now, channel your inner porn star."

Feeling too exposed, she moved the chemise so it again covered her fully. Then she looked at Mark from under her eyelashes and smiled as she lifted her hands to cup her breasts.

He hissed in response, then disappeared behind the camera.

"That's the spirit," he said. "I'm going to start the countdown now."

By the time Mark said "action" she was already turned on. She let her eyes flutter closed and sank deep into the alternative reality she wished she was living in right now. The one where Mark abandoned his camera and came to kneel at her side, gently caressing her breasts and stomach before finding his way lower, to the heated mound that hid beneath the black lace of her panties.

She moaned loudly for Mark's benefit and grabbed the yogurt container from the bedside table. Running her hands up and down its smooth surface, she tried to imagine it was Mark's penis she was stroking.

She let her moans come faster as she pictured Mark putting his mouth to work in her hot wet folds, flicking and sucking and bringing her right to the brink…

"Oh, yes," she groaned. "Oh, please. Oh, God…"

She was wondering how much longer she should continue when she felt a rough, masculine hand fumbling with her undies.

Opening her eyes, she saw Mark hovering over her, desire blazing out of his eyes.

"Oh, Mark," she breathed, seeing that victory was within her grasp. "Oh, please. Please make me come."

A primal growl rumbled in his chest as Mark tore the black lace panties off her body. Seconds later he was plunging a finger deep into her core, a ferocious look on his face. Although he was only touching her in that one sensitive place his gaze pinned her down, making her feel strangely, wonderfully helpless. This wasn't a man giving a woman what she wanted. It was a man taking what he needed—and she was happy to give it to him. Feeling the delicious pressure mount inside, she let her knees slide out to the side, giving him even better access.

"Come for me," he said gruffly. "I want to see you do it."

As soon as the words were out of his mouth she felt herself doing exactly that, her body clenching around his hand in an orgasm so intense that it left her shivering and shaking.

Quickly Mark shrugged out of his own clothes and fumbled with a condom, hands shaking as he rolled it on.

Desperate to feel him inside her, she scooted to the edge

of the bed and tried to wrap her legs around him, but he shook his head.

"No. Not that way. Flip," he said, still using that strangely authoritative tone.

She just looked at him, confused.

"Like this," he commanded, rolling her on to her stomach and propping her up on her hands and knees. Becky found herself looking down at the bed, unable to see what was going on behind her. The suspense thrilled in her blood as she waited, her whole body crying out for his touch.

Suddenly she felt his hands on her hips, grabbing the tender skin possessively.

"I want you to feel how deep I can go," he growled from somewhere behind and above her, his manhood nudging at her sensitive folds. "I want you to know that it's me, reaching into the center of you, making you mine."

He slid deep inside her core, burying himself to the hilt. She gasped, loving the feeling of complete possession, wanting him to take even more. He was claiming her, and every cell of her body celebrated, wanting to feel his imprint on her.

She rocked back against him, signaling her silent acceptance. He slammed into her, filling her to capacity, his hard thick length rubbing against all her most sensitive spots, and as he did something primal roared to life inside her. This man was hers, and she was his, in every way that mattered.

He reached down and grabbed her hair in his hands, pulling her head back. "You. Are. Mine," he said, thrusting even harder, and she shattered into a million tiny pieces, her orgasm hitting her more strongly than any ever had.

With a tortured-sounding moan he let himself go, shuddering as he came apart inside her. Then he collapsed sideways on to the bed, their bodies still connected.

She followed him down, breathing hard, trying to wrap

her head around what had just happened. She had intended to get through his defenses and get him to touch her. And, boy, had she succeeded. If only he hadn't managed to get through so many of hers, as well…

Something monumental had happened here tonight. She only hoped she had the strength to cope with whatever came next.

Suddenly exhausted, she closed her eyes and started to drift into sleep.

"I don't think we're going to be able to use that take," a sleepy voice said behind her.

Alarm bells rang in her head. "You filmed that?"

He laughed. "No. Of course not. That would get us both fired."

"Oh. Good," she said and yawned.

"Close your eyes, Sleeping Beauty," he said. "It's time to rest. It'll all still be here in the morning."

That sounded like the best idea she had ever heard.

The next thing she knew it was morning. She yawned and stretched, reaching for the warm male body she knew must still be beside her. Except…it wasn't. His side of the bed was empty and cold.

She sat up, alarmed. "M-Mark?"

Surely he hadn't run again. Not after what had happened last night. "Mark? Are you here?"

For a long moment there was silence and she began to panic. He couldn't be gone. They needed to talk. She needed to make sure none of those last scenes had been captured on film.

"Mark?" she yelled. "Where are you?"

Still nothing.

She was fumbling for her flimsy excuse for a nightgown, swearing quietly to herself, when she heard the suite's door open. "Mark?"

"Yeah, babe. I'm here," he said, coming to stand in the bedroom door. "I just went to get you some coffee. Venti soy, right?"

Relief flooded through her system. "Yep. I'm impressed that you remembered," she said, padding over to where he stood.

He handed her cup to her, then swooped down to give her a tender kiss. "I try to remember everything about the people who are important to me," he said.

Important? She was important to him? That was a switch. Suddenly she felt vaguely ashamed of her behavior the night before.

"Look, I know you didn't want to be physical anymore," she said, looking down. "So if you want to forget what happened last night I understand."

He sighed.

"I couldn't forget it if I wanted to," he said. "Becky, look at me."

Reluctantly, she looked up, expecting to see derision in his eyes. Instead there was only happiness.

"Look, I know I've been an ass. And I don't blame you if you want to forget *me,*" he said. "But that's not what I want."

"It's not?" she asked.

"No. Truth is, I did nothing for those three days other than wish I could be with you, and laugh with you, and touch you. I was useless. You had it right all along."

"Well, of course I did," she said, trying to catch up to him. "What was I right about, exactly?"

"There's no harm in what we're doing. We're just making the best of a crazy situation and enjoying ourselves along the way."

"So you want...?"

"I want you. For as long as we're both into it. No strings, like you said. Just fun."

Just fun. That was definitely what she had wanted. But,

remembering the way her heart had flipped the night before, Becky was pretty sure she was getting into deeper waters.

But he didn't need to know that.

"Okay, you're on," she said, injecting a smile into her voice. "But if you freak out on me again, I reserve the right to do serious damage."

He raised an eyebrow. "What kind of damage?"

She gently caressed his penis through his pants, bringing it roaring back to life.

"I'm not going to tell you. Where's the fun in that? But it would be in an area that's precious to you."

She waited for the shocked expression to cross his face, then turned her back.

"Last one in the shower's a rotten egg," she called as she pulled the gown free of her body and headed for the bathroom.

Seconds later, Mark sprinted by. "Nope, last one in the shower's the first to get taken advantage of," he said, laughing.

At that, Becky slowed. She'd never heard a better reason to take her time.

Becky plopped down on to the red vinyl seat across from Jessie, unable to keep the smile from her face.

"Wow, you look happy," Jessie said. "Did Mark suddenly drop out of the competition?"

Becky laughed. "Of course not!"

"Did David finally come to his senses, realize you're the most amazing copywriter who ever lived, and promote you?"

Becky could only snort. "As if."

"Did he have a heart attack and die and leave the agency to you?"

"Who?"

"David, of course," Jessie said. "Who else?"

"Oh," Becky said. "No. Which is good. I wouldn't want someone's death on my conscience. Besides, I want David to have to admit that I'm talented and worthy of promotion before he kicks the bucket. If he doesn't, I may have to chase him into the afterlife."

"All right, then, I give up. Why are you so smiley? Did you forget you have the biggest pitch of your life in less than two weeks?"

"I wish I could," Becky said, scooting to the window side of the booth and stretching her legs out on the seat. "But there's not a chance of that."

Their favorite waitress bustled over with a gap-toothed smile. "Well, if it isn't my two favorite advertising ladies," she said. "You're looking good today."

Becky giggled up at the matronly woman. "Thank you, Rachel. Your uniform looks pretty fetching today, too!"

Rachel cocked an eyebrow at Becky. "You look different," she said. "All glowy and stuff. Are you in love? Are you finally going to bring me some eye candy? We could use some good-looking man flesh to pretty up the place around here."

Becky felt herself pale. "In love? N-no. Farthest thing from it. I haven't got time for anything like that," she sputtered.

"Mmm-hmm," Rachel said. "Whatever you say. Should I bring you two the usual?"

Becky felt her stomach flip uncomfortably at the idea of pancakes.

"I'll just have a piece of dry toast, if you don't mind. And maybe some tea?"

Rachel gave her another piercing look, but just nodded and turned to Jessie. "How 'bout you? Are you going all rabbitlike on me, too?"

Jessie shook her head. "Nope. In fact, you can bring me

her stack of pancakes, if you want. Working all these hours has made me hungry!"

"You got it," Rachel said, and walked away.

"So what did you do this weekend?" Becky asked, desperately trying to deflect the question she knew was coming.

"Doesn't matter. Right now, I'm interrogating my best friend. *Are* you? In love?"

"No," Becky said, "I most definitely am not. I'm making plenty of love, but not falling into it."

"Ah. So you and Mark are at it again, huh? That didn't take long."

"No," Becky said, "It didn't." Even though it had felt like an eternity.

"And how is it? The sex? Still good?"

"It's...amazing."

Truth was, since the night of the videos they'd spent almost every nonworking hour together—and some working ones. On Friday she'd cooked him dinner in her tiny apartment and fed him dessert in bed.

Then, on Saturday, he'd taken her to his favorite Vietnamese restaurant, fed her drinks in his favorite dive bar and introduced her to the dirty high that was sex in a public bathroom.

And they'd spent yesterday in the production studio, editing videos and teasing each other. It had been the most amazing weekend she could remember having in a very long time.

"Hey, space cadet?"

Becky blinked, bringing herself back to the present. "Yeah?"

"You sure this is just a fling?"

"Yes. Positive," Becky said, trying to convince herself it was true. "We both know the rules. We're having a lot of fun."

"Hmm," Jessie said. "It's just I haven't seen you look this happy…well, ever. Maybe you should rethink where you're headed with this thing. This guy's good for you."

Becky glared at her friend. "No. When this pitch is over, this thing with Mark and me ends, too. I'll be too busy after I get promoted to bother with a man."

"All right, you know I support you, girl. But there's more to life than work."

Unfortunately that was something Becky was becoming all too aware of. Good thing she knew that Mark had no intention of starting a "real" relationship…

Otherwise she might find herself tempted to take Jessie's words to heart.

Mark hit Stop on the remote and flipped the lights back on, pride snaking through his belly. The videos had turned out well. Really well. If David didn't like them—well, he was an ass.

"So what do you think?" he asked.

David blinked slowly for a moment, silent. Then he smiled.

"I think you two deserve congratulations. If Eden doesn't sign on the dotted line after seeing these, then nothing will convince them. These are deal-closers," David said.

Mark looked at Becky and grinned. "I'm glad you like them. We worked hard to put these together."

David looked at Becky.

"I had no idea you had it in you to act like that, my dear," he said, leering slightly. "If you didn't work for me, I'd be tempted to ask you out for dinner."

Mark felt his hackles go up. Instinctively he moved closer to Becky, even though he knew she didn't need protecting.

"Wow, David, that's quite the compliment," she said. "But if you asked me I'd say no. I don't date married men."

David flushed. "Well, uh, I was just speaking hypothetically," he stuttered.

Mark decided it was time to step in.

"I'm glad you liked the videos," he said. "But we've got a lot more work to do. Far too much to think about even hypothetical dates."

David took the out he'd been offered.

"I'm sure you do," he said as he headed for the door. "So, uh, I'll leave you to it! Keep up the good work."

After the door closed Becky kissed him on the cheek.

"Thank you, Magic Man."

"No need to thank me. You were doing a fine job of putting him in his place."

"Yeah, but if you hadn't spoken up it may have come to blows," she said. "And I don't feel like going to jail today." She stretched and yawned. "But you know what? I *do* feel like I need a break."

"One that involves taking your clothes off?" he asked, waggling his eyebrows suggestively. He hadn't had her in his arms in…almost eighteen hours. They were overdue.

Becky laughed. "Nice try. Actually, I'd like to go on a picnic."

"A picnic?" That was definitely not what he'd had in mind.

"Yeah. Have you been outside today? It's beautiful," she said, opening up the window shades.

He turned to look outside. Sure enough, the sun was shining, and if he looked down he could see that the people below seemed to be wearing warm weather gear.

"Well," he said slowly, "it has been several days since I've seen the sun. But I have to admit I've never been on an actual picnic. How does this work?"

"You're a picnic virgin? At your age? Huh! Leave it to me, big boy. I'll take good care of you," she said, smiling.

* * *

A short time later they were outside in the warm October sunshine.

"First we need to get some eats," Becky said, pulling him into an upscale bodega. Grabbing a shopping basket, she headed for the dairy section. "Cheese," she said. "We need cheese."

"How 'bout this?" Mark asked, holding up a package of precut artisan cheeses.

"Perfect," she said.

"Next up, bread," she added, placing a warm baguette in the basket. "And these strawberries will do nicely." Then she headed to the deli case. "Are you hungry? Because I could really go for some meat."

She motioned to the butcher, and soon a hefty packet of sliced deli meats joined the treats in their basket.

"Oh, and wine! But I'll let you choose."

Mark grabbed a bottle of Chardonnay, adding a bar of dark chocolate for good measure. He felt himself getting absurdly excited about their upcoming picnic. It was the kind of thing he'd always wanted to do with his mother. But she'd never had the time or the inclination.

Becky found him and he snapped out of his reverie.

"Ready?"

He nodded.

They paid and rejoined the happy throng outside, everyone seemingly intent on getting the most out of what could be the season's last warm day.

"We've got our food. Now where to?" he asked.

"That's for me to know…"

"And me to find out?" he finished.

"Yep." She grabbed his hand and tugged. "This way."

They walked in companionable silence, enjoying the warm breeze and rambunctious crowd. A toddler raced by, giggling gleefully.

"Josh! Josh, get back here, or so help me God..." a frantic voice yelled from somewhere behind them.

Mark jogged forward and grabbed the hood of the child's sweatshirt.

"Hey, little man, I think you're forgetting someone," he said, smiling.

Scooping him up, he carried the boy back to his petrified mother.

"I take it this is Josh?"

She took the boy from his arms, relief flooding her face.

"Yes. Oh, thank you. He was right there and then...I thought I'd lost him!"

"Hey, no problem," Mark said, squeezing her shoulder. Tapping Josh's nose with his finger, he admonished him. "No more running for you, young man. Don't you know that there are alligators in the sewers, just waiting for a tasty morsel like you to run by?"

The boy's eyes grew wide.

"Really?"

"Really. Your mom will tell you all about it," he said, and jogged back to Becky.

"That was really nice of you," she said, a thoughtful look on her face.

"I am the child of a single mom—or at least I was when I was young. I remember doing things like that to her. This was my penance."

"That's right. You said your mom didn't remarry until you were a little older?"

"Marry. Not remarry. I was born a bastard."

Becky winced. "That's pretty strong language. I'm sure she never thought of you that way."

Mark smiled bitterly. "Oh, I'm sure she did. Her pet name for me was Mr. Mistake. I pretty much ruined her life."

Lord knew, he had enough memories of his mother looking tired and worried, massaging her temples at the kitchen table.

Whatever you do, Mark, she'd say, bending over her calculator, *don't have kids. Life's hard enough as it is.*

He certainly never intended to. Especially since he had no desire to get involved enough with a woman to make a child. No relationships, no children, he chanted to himself. No relationships, no…

Becky squeezed his hand, bringing him out of his daydream.

"I'll bet you were her favorite mistake," she said. "You're definitely mine."

He smiled, which he was sure was the effect she had intended. "Oh, so I'm a mistake, am I?" he asked, one eyebrow raised.

"Oh, most definitely. One I enjoy making over and over again," she answered, her hand sliding into his front pocket and caressing his suddenly hard penis. "In fact, I'd like to do it again this afternoon."

"Mmm," he growled. "Keep doing that and you'll be making it in the next alley I can find."

"Now, now," she said. "Have a little patience. We're almost there."

"I guess we are," he said, suddenly realizing they'd arrived at Central Park.

A short while later she tugged at his hand again, urging him off the blacktopped path they'd been following and onto a carpet of green grass.

They were standing on a gentle slope. At the bottom was a peaceful lake, its waters reflecting the blazing reds, golds and oranges of the trees that surrounded it.

"This is amazing," he said.

"Isn't it? It's just about my favorite spot in the whole park."

She sat down under a fiery red maple tree and started unloading their picnic.

"What do you want to try first?" she asked, looking up at him.

Mark sat down next to her and gathered her up in his arms. "You," he said, and kissed her.

As always, the gentle kiss he'd intended to give her quickly morphed into something more. Her mouth opened under his and he moaned.

"Becky," he said, nibbling at her neck, "you make me crazy."

"Mmm," she murmured, tilting her head to give him better access to the sensitive pulse point, "I could say the same thing about you."

Mark glanced up. For the moment, at least, they were alone. He pushed his hand underneath her brown corduroy skirt, his fingers seeking the place his mouth wanted to go.

He stroked the edges of her cotton panties and said, "I want to make you come."

"Do you think it's safe?"

"Don't worry. Nobody will see."

Panting slightly, she nodded. "All right. If you're sure."

"I am," he said, scooping her up into his lap.

He stroked her silken folds through her underpants, smiling when she moaned. He loved that it was so easy to get her going. Slowly he increased the pace, his heart rate increasing as her breath sped up. Finally, when he couldn't take it anymore, he reached underneath to caress the tiny knob of pleasure at her core. In seconds she began writhing silently on his lap as she climaxed, then collapsed against his chest. He smiled with satisfaction, knowing she'd never trust anyone else enough to let go like that in public.

"You are amazing," she sighed.

"I thought the word was *magic?*"

"That, too."

He lay back on the grass, keeping her snuggled securely against his chest.

Looking up at the scarlet leaves above them, he sighed contentedly. "You were right," he said. "This was a fantastic idea."

"I usually am." She grinned.

"True enough."

He closed his eyes and relaxed, letting the sound of the wind in the trees lull him to sleep.

He woke up with a start when his phone burst into life.

Groggily, he reached into his pocket and grabbed it, hitting the Talk button without even looking to see who it was.

"Hello?" he said sleepily.

"Forget hello. Where the hell *are* you?" David said. He sounded furious.

"Becky and I decided to take advantage of the nice weather and do a little brainstorming off-site," he said.

"Well, get your asses back here. The client has decided to move up the presentation by an entire week. That means we have three days."

Crap.

"We're on our way," he said, and hung up.

"What was that about?" Becky asked, blinking sleepily.

"Eden has moved the presentation up. We've got three days."

"What?" she said, rubbing her face sleepily. "Okay… okay, we can do this. We just need to get our asses in gear."

She stood and gathered up their food.

"We never got to eat," he said sadly.

"No worries. I have a feeling the food's going to come in handy. Sounds like we're not going to be leaving the office much for the next little while."

"You're right about that," he said, leaning down to give her one last kiss.

"What was that for?"

"I don't think we're going to have much time for fun and games," he said. "That's to tide you over."

The next three days passed in a caffeine-fueled blur. Mark and Becky worked nonstop, pausing only to sleep when it became absolutely necessary.

Their teams toiled beside them, and against all odds they created a stunningly good campaign. When it was over, Mark was proud of the work they had done—and even more proud of the woman who had worked at his side.

She was the heart and soul of the team, doling out encouragement when needed, praise when deserved, and tissues whenever the occasion seemed to call for it.

It was obvious that everyone loved and respected her, and Mark realized that if there was any justice in the world he'd have no shot at the creative director title. She deserved it far more than he did.

Mark had sent her to get some rest and was just packing the last of the boards away when David found him.

"You've done great work here, Mark," he said.

"Thank you, but it was a team effort. I couldn't have done it alone."

"Still, I've been watching you and I've been impressed by what I've seen. You have the makings of an outstanding creative director."

Mark couldn't help but be pleased by the praise.

"Thank you. I hope to be when my time comes."

"I have a feeling your time will come tomorrow," David said. "There's still a promotion up for grabs, remember?"

"I do, but I don't know how you're going to decide who gets it. Becky has worked just as hard as I have."

"She has," David agreed. "But I'm just not sure I sense the same potential for leadership in her."

Obviously the man was blind.

"Are you kidding? The team would follow her right up to the gates of hell—and even beyond—if she asked them to."

"You're right. The power of a pretty face can't be underestimated," David said. "Don't sweat it. I'll find the right place for her."

Mark stared hard at David's retreating back. How could the man be so willfully obtuse? He had one of the industry's most talented women working for him and he didn't appreciate her at all.

One thing was for sure. When he was in charge things would be different.

CHAPTER EIGHT

AS THEY RODE the elevator to the twenty-sixth floor of Eden's headquarters Becky checked her reflection in the shiny metal door, nervously tucking a stray hair behind her ear and checking her teeth for lipstick for the hundredth time.

"Babe, don't worry," Mark said. "You look great."

She knew she did. Her hair shone like gold against the navy blue of her suit jacket. The A-line skirt flattered her curves, and her heels were a to-die-for shade of ruby-red—not to mention dangerously high.

"We're a pretty good-looking team, if I do say so myself." She grinned, enjoying the sudden rush of adrenaline that flooded through her veins.

"You better believe it. Flash those pearly whites at them and they'll be ours before we even say a word."

"I hope you're right," Becky said.

"I know I am," Mark answered, bending down to give her a quick peck on the mouth.

Just then the elevator doors dinged open and Mark straightened.

"You ready?"

"As ready as I'll ever be," she replied.

They made their way through an empty oak-paneled lobby and headed for the conference room labeled Agency Pitch.

They hesitated outside and Mark squeezed her hand, a question on his face. She winked up at him and whispered, "Let's do this thing."

He nodded and stepped inside. Becky followed.

There were twelve business-suited men and women sitting around a long oak table. They were making polite conversation while noshing on coffee and doughnuts, but all chatter ceased when they noticed Becky and Mark standing there.

"Ah, there you are," David said, rising from his chair. "Ladies and gentlemen, this is Becky Logan and Mark Powers, the creative masterminds behind today's presentation. Between the two of them they've won more than a dozen major advertising awards and worked for some of the hottest brands around. I selected them for this project specifically because I knew they had the fresh attitude and unexpected creative flair you need. I know normally we'd do a round of introductions, but we have a lot to cover, so if it's okay with you I'd like to just let them dive in."

There was murmured assent from around the table.

"Great," David said. "Mark, Becky—take it away."

Mark looked at Becky and she nodded. They'd already agreed that he would start the presentation.

He took a deep breath and strode to the head of the table.

"Good morning, ladies and gentlemen," Mark boomed, smiling at the multitude of gray suits in the room. "I hope you brought an extra pair of socks, because we're about to blow the ones you're wearing right off."

"That's right," Becky chimed in. "The campaign we're about to present to you is like nothing you have ever seen. It will change the way business is done in your industry—and make your competition green with jealousy."

"She's not kidding, folks. Tell them how you came up with the idea."

"Well, I was sitting at my desk late one night, thinking, *Now, why would a woman buy our yogurt? What does it do for her?* What do you guys think? Why does a woman buy yogurt?"

A tall redhead raised her hand.

"Yes?" Becky said, waving in her direction.

"Well, because it tastes good," the woman answered.

"Yeah, it does—but so does ice cream. Anyone else?"

"Well, she buys *our* yogurt because it's all natural, high in protein and low in fat," a gray-haired man said.

"Ah-ha, now we're getting closer to the truth. Women buy yogurt because it makes them feel good about themselves. Not only are they making a healthy choice, but they're making a decision even the most critical part of them can appreciate."

"So you're saying we should market our yogurt as a diet aid? That's already been done," the redhead said.

"No, not as a diet aid," Mark said. "As a portal to another world—one where every woman achieves her version of perfection. Show them the concept, Becky."

Becky uncovered the first board.

A woman sat in a classic yogini pose, looking calm and Zen, while surrounded by screaming kids and spilled milk.

"Eden. The snack for the perfect you."

Over the next hour the two of them bantered back and forth effortlessly, trapping the client in a silken web. When the presentation was over, everyone at the table clapped.

The graying middle-aged man who had chimed in at the beginning stood up.

"I'm sold. David, get your team moving, because I want to get this campaign in market by January one."

"You've got it, Larry," David said, clapping the paunchy man on his back. "We look forward to it."

"Great. And, just to be clear, I want these two in charge," he said, pointing at Becky and Mark. "No one else. Don't foist me off on your B team—you hear me?"

David smiled his sleazy salesman grin. "Not to worry, my man. After all the work this team has put in, we wouldn't dream of giving it to anyone else."

The man nodded his satisfaction. Turning his attention to Becky and Mark, he said, "I look forward to getting to know you two better. I know we're going to do wonderful things together."

Becky gave him her brightest smile, her heart soaring. "We certainly will. Thank you for your confidence in us."

"Yes, thanks," Mark chimed in. "We'll try to knock your socks off every time we meet."

"I'm counting on it," said Larry. "Now, if you'll excuse me, I have some business to take care of. Where's Mary?"

A tall woman rushed to his side. "Yes, sir?"

"Is that other creative team still waiting downstairs?"

"Yes, they are. They're scheduled to begin presenting in fifteen minutes."

"Send them home. I have no use for them now. Can't stand their creative director anyway."

"Right away, sir," she said. Then she turned her attention to David. "Can you see yourselves out? I really need to take care of this."

David nodded. "Of course. We'll get everything cleared up and be on our way."

"Great," she said, and hurried out.

Becky busied herself with the boards so no one would see her triumphant smile. Inside, though, she was jumping up and down with glee.

Take that, Pence, she thought. *You've just been schooled by your former student. Booyah!*

When the last bigwig had left the room, David came over and clapped them both on the back.

"Well, team, I believe congratulations are in order. You pulled it off!" He looked down at the gold Rolex on his wrist. "Let's see. It's noon now. Meet me in the large conference room at four and we'll make it official."

"Make what official?" Becky blurted.

David gave her a sly smile. "I guess you'll have to show up to find out."

He waved goodbye and left, leaving them alone in the conference room.

Mark held up his hand. "High five," he said, grinning. "We did it."

She slapped it enthusiastically.

"What do you think David will do? Larry specifically said he wants both of us on the team."

"I have no idea," Mark said. "And I'm not really in the mood to worry about it. Let's go have us a Midwestern carnivore kind of lunch—and charge it to the company."

"That sounds fantastic," she said. "But let's go see if we can find Pence's team and gloat first."

The moment they stepped off the elevator Becky heard the sound of raised voices. One definitely belonged to Pence.

Becky grabbed Mark's hand and followed the squawks into the central reception area.

"What do you mean, he won't see us? I flew my entire team from Detroit for this meeting!" Pence sputtered, his face flushing beet-red as he gesticulated wildly. "I demand that he make good on his promise to meet with us!"

Mary was doing her best to calm him. "I'm sorry, Mr. Britton, but there's nothing I can do. Mr. Richards has left for the day."

"Left for the day? How can that be? I—we…"

Becky knew she'd never have a better chance to exact her revenge. Stepping forward, she said, "Mary? I'm sorry to interrupt, but can I steal you for a second?"

Relief flooded the other woman's face. "Yes, Becky? What can I do for you?"

"David had to leave, but he wanted me to make sure to tell you that he'll be emailing over some contracts later this afternoon. In order to stick to the timeline Mr. Richards has requested we're going to need to move fast."

"Of course. I'll be on the lookout for them. Tell David he'll have the signed contracts by the end of the week."

"Wait. What?" Pence squawked, his blue eyes flashing with anger as he moved to stand in front of Becky. "Are you telling me *your* team won the business?"

"As a matter of fact I'm not telling you anything at all. You can read all about it in the next issue of AdWorld."

"You little..." Pence said, rage suffusing his face.

Before he could finish the thought, Mark stepped forward.

"Is this your old boss, Becky?"

She nodded. "The one and only."

"I've heard a lot about you," he said, extending his hand. "None of it good."

Pence reluctantly shook it. "And you are...?"

"Mark Powers. Becky's teammate. You have no idea what you missed out on when you let her go, buddy. This woman is brilliant."

Pence's already scarlet face turned even redder.

"I don't know what she's told you, but it's almost certainly not what actually happened," he said.

"I'm not interested in your opinion," Mark said. "Come on, Becky, let's get out of here."

But Becky wasn't done yet.

Turning back to Pence, she smiled sweetly. "If you get canned, give me a call. We might be able to find a job for you. In our mail room."

Then she turned on her heel and swaggered out, leaving Mark to follow.

When they were clear of the building he pulled her to him and kissed her soundly.

"That," he said between kisses, "was amazing."

"I know," she said smugly. "You have no idea how good

that felt. It's like a million-pound weight has been lifted off my back."

"Wanna celebrate…in bed?"

"I do. But not until we know for sure what we're celebrating," she said, stepping backward out of his arms. If David announced he was giving the promotion to Mark, she didn't want to hear the news while still tingling from his touch.

"Okay, then. Still up for lunch?"

She shook her head. "I'd like to be alone for a little while. It's been a big morning. I need some time to process it, you know?"

He nodded, a sad smile on his face. "I get it. See you back at the office, then?"

"Yep," she said, then reached up to give him one last melting kiss.

"What was that for?"

"Just a little something to tide you over," she said. Silently she added, *And something for me to remember you by.*

Mark jogged around the corner, his dress shoes slipping on the polished cement floor. If there was one meeting he didn't want to be late for it was this one.

Once the frosted glass doors were in sight he stopped for a second to catch his breath and straighten his tie.

This was it. If he got this promotion he could finally feel as if he'd made it. That he'd gotten where he had in his career because he was talented—not because his stepfather had greased the wheels. His mother might even be a little bit proud of him. Maybe she'd stop thinking of him as a mistake.

Taking a deep breath, he stepped through the conference room doors.

It was crowded. And hot. Everyone in the whole agency

seemed to be there, and the air was quickly growing stale. David stood at the head of the big table, with Becky on his right.

"There you are, Mark. We were beginning to wonder if you'd gone off somewhere to celebrate without us."

"Just staying true to form. You know how I like to make an entrance," he joked.

Becky rolled her eyes at him.

"Yep," she said. "He's the diva on this team. I'm the brains and the brawn."

The assembled crowd laughed appreciatively.

"All right, enough monkey business," David said. "Come on up here and we'll get this show on the road."

Mark made his way to the front of the room, taking his place at David's left.

Once the audience had stilled, David launched into his speech.

"As you all know, we delivered our pitch to Eden this morning. Mark and Becky led the presentation, and I must admit they did a fantastic job. They had the client eating out of their hands. They even got a standing ovation."

There was a smattering of applause in the room.

"In fact," David said, "the client bought into the campaign on the spot. We're the new marketing partner for Eden Yogurt—and about to be two hundred and fifty million dollars richer as an agency!"

The room broke out into riotous applause as their colleagues cheered their victory.

"That's not all," David continued. "As you may remember, Becky and Mark have been involved in a competition of sorts. The prize was a creative director title and a hefty bonus."

The room stilled as everyone waited for the next part of the announcement.

"But choosing one over the other has proved to be surprisingly difficult. They're both incredibly skilled creative geniuses. They both worked on the winning concept from beginning to end. And they both gained the respect and admiration of the client."

Mark drew in a breath and held it.

"So in the end I decided to create a new type of position. One that gives them each their due. Mark and Becky, you're now creative codirectors. You'll function as a creative director team, splitting the responsibilities for the Eden account according to your skillsets."

Mark blinked, trying to connect the dots.

Next to him, Becky said, "So there's no winner or loser? We're both getting promoted?"

"That's right," David said. "Eden is a new kind of account for us. It's only right that a new type of team heads it up."

The room exploded with cheers.

Becky shrieked happily and threw her arms around David. "Thank you," she said. "Thank you so much!"

He chuckled and patted her back uncomfortably.

"I'm the one who should be thanking you, my dear. You've just secured my retirement. Which brings me to my last announcement… If this were a television show I'd have a giant check sitting here. But, since it's not, you'll just have to make do with these regular-size ones."

He turned to Mark.

"One fifty-thousand-dollar check for you," he said, and, to Becky, "One fifty-thousand-dollar check for you."

Stunned, Mark looked down at the check in his hand. This was really happening. The check was his. The job was his. And, he thought, looking at Becky's laughing countenance as she accepted congratulations from her friends, at least for now the girl was his.

He was surprised to discover that it was that last ingredient that made him the happiest.

Maybe it was time to rethink the no-relationship clause.

* * *

By the time Becky managed to break free from her excited colleagues and escape to their office, darkness was falling over the city.

She closed the door and leaned against it, reveling in the blessed quiet.

She jumped when Mark's voice rang out in the darkness.

"Congratulations, creative codirector," he said. "You did good today."

"Mark? Where are you?"

"Just admiring the view," he said, clicking on a lamp by the windows. "And enjoying the fact that I'll get to look at it every day from now on."

Becky crossed over to where he was standing. Time to reintroduce reality.

"What if I want this office?"

He blinked. "What?"

"Now that we're both creative directors, or at least codirectors, David will probably give us each our own office. What if I decide I want to keep this one?"

"I guess I assumed we'd continue to share," Mark said. "Since we're heading up the same account and all."

"I doubt it," she said. In fact she hoped not. It would be almost impossible to keep her distance from him—something she knew she had to start doing—if they were in each other's physical space all day.

"Do you want your own office?" Mark asked, a dark look on his face.

She sighed. "Yes and no. Mark, these last few weeks have been fun, but we've known from the beginning that this couldn't last. Remember what you said?"

"I said that we could both go our own ways after this thing between us had run its course."

"Right," she said. "No harm, no foul."

"But, Becky," he said, looking deep into her eyes, "I

don't think it *has* run its course. I'm having a lot of fun with you—even when our clothes are on. Let's not give up yet."

Uh-oh. Unless she was very mistaken, he was talking about more than the occasional sexual romp.

"That was never the deal, Mark. You don't do relationships, remember?"

He sighed and ran his fingers through his dark hair. "No, Becky, I don't. Or at least I never have. But this… It's different somehow."

She knew exactly what he was talking about. Somewhere along the way they had crossed the line from being sex buddies to…something more. Something that scared her even to think about.

"I know," she said. "But we can't keep going on as we are—hooking up in the office on the sly and slipping out of the building when no one's looking. We're in charge now. Role models. We're going to have to try to act like we realize that."

He wrapped his arms around her and pulled her close. "Well, what if we try something different? Something normal and grown-up-ish. Like, you know, going out on actual dates. And spending the night together whenever we want, rather than heading home after a hookup. That could be fun."

"Mark…" she whispered. "What you're talking about sounds an awful lot like a relationship."

"I know," he said. "But I bet we can make it work."

"You and your bets," she said, smiling. "Nothing is worth doing unless you can bet on it."

He grinned and lowered his lips to hers.

"So what do you think?" he said. "Are you in?"

"I don't know. I'll think about it."

Then he claimed her with his mouth and she stopped thinking at all.

The next thing she knew someone was knocking. She

jumped backward—but not before the door opened, admitting David.

His eyes darted back and forth between her and Mark, taking in their slightly disheveled clothing and flushed faces.

"David," she said. "We were just, uh, I mean, we were—"

"We were just cementing the official end of our feud slash competitive relationship with a hug," Mark broke in.

"Oh. I see," David said, twitching his tie. "Well, that makes sense. Especially since you're going to be working together every day. It's important to present a united front."

"Exactly," Becky said, glancing at Mark.

"Well, I was just coming in to congratulate you one more time," David replied. "Make sure you get some rest this weekend. We're going to hit it hard on Monday. Becky, you'll be moving into the office next door to this one—Fred Sutherland's old digs."

She nodded, relieved that he seemed to be buying their story.

"Sounds good," she said.

"See you Monday," Mark chimed in.

"Right you are," David said, giving them one last suspicious glance. "Have a good one."

When the door was once again closed Becky whirled on Mark. "That," she hissed, "is why an 'us' is not a good idea. I just got promoted. I don't want to get fired."

"I don't remember signing anything that said we couldn't date coworkers."

"Maybe not, but I'm sure David wouldn't approve of the two of us getting together. And you know how tough it is for him to treat me like a creative professional. He'd find a way to use our relationship as a way to discredit me."

"I think you're being a little tough on the guy. All he cares about is the bottom line. And you just tripled his income. I don't think he's going to give you a hard time about anything."

Becky shook her head. It was no use. Mark would never understand how tough this business was for women. Or how biased David was against female employees.

"Well, whatever. Only time will tell," she said. "But I just don't think he could handle the thought of us as both a couple and a working team."

If she was being honest, she wasn't sure if she could, either.

"Just promise me you'll think about it," Mark said.

She sighed and stood on her tiptoes to kiss him goodbye. What she wouldn't give to be able to throw caution to the winds and just say yes. But she had to start focusing on her career again.

"I will," she agreed. "But don't expect me to change my mind."

CHAPTER NINE

BECKY WAS JUST sitting down with a steaming pot pie and a glass of her favorite Pinot Grigio when her cell phone began to whistle cheerfully.

It was her mother.

Becky stared at the screen. Should she answer it? Probably. If she didn't, she'd just keep calling back.

"Hi, Mom."

"Well, there you are. I was beginning to wonder if you were lying dead in an alley somewhere."

"Don't be so dramatic, Mom. It hasn't been that long since we talked."

"I haven't heard from you since you called to tell me you got home safely from the conference! That was almost a month ago."

Surely it hadn't been that long? But, now that she thought about it, maybe it had. She had considered picking up the phone on countless occasions, but when she'd thought about everything that was going on, and how impossible it would be to explain to her mom, she never had.

"I'm sorry, Mom. Things have been really busy at work."

"Work, work, work. That's all you ever talk about. When are you going to give me something to brag about to the ladies in my book club?"

"Well, actually, something pretty huge happened today," Becky said, suddenly eager to tell her mom. "I got promoted. To creative director."

There was a brief silence.

"That's nice, dear. Does that mean you'll be able to afford to come home more often?"

"I don't know. We haven't discussed salary yet. But I did get a really big bonus."

"Maybe you should use it to buy a place in a better neighborhood. I worry about you, you know. It doesn't seem safe, especially with those tattooed hippies wandering around at all hours of the day and night."

"Mom. I live in Greenwich Village, not Hell's Kitchen. This is a great neighborhood."

"I'm sure it is, but I'd feel much better if you didn't live right in the city like that. There's so much crime."

Becky smacked her forehead with her palm.

"We've been over this a hundred times. I moved to New York because I wanted to live in the city. Not in some cookie-cutter house in the suburbs."

Now it was her mother's turn to sigh. "I know, dear. I know. I just wish you'd move past this wild phase of yours and settle down with someone nice."

Becky snorted. Wild phase, indeed. "I'm only twenty-nine. There's no rush."

"That's what you think, dear. But once you hit thirty, your best baby-making years are behind you. I don't want you to end up in some infertility clinic, trying to get your tired eggs to work."

"I know. I've read every article you've ever emailed me on the subject."

Her mother continued as if she hadn't heard.

"You know, your cousin is pregnant again."

"Which one?"

"Tiffany. This will be her third."

"Well, tell her I said congratulations."

"You could come for the baby shower and tell her yourself."

"I'd rather stick needles in my eye," she muttered.

"I heard that," her mother said, sighing loudly. "Well, I'll let you go. I'm sure you have far better things to do than talk to your mother on a Friday night."

If only, Becky thought. Out loud, she said, "All right. Well, I'll talk to you soon, Mom. Love you."

"Love you, too. Remember to take the pepper spray I bought you if you go out."

"I will."

"And never leave your drink unattended."

"Okay."

"And…"

At long last her mother hung up. Becky flung herself backward on the chaise. Any other parent would be thrilled to hear their child had just gotten promoted. But not her mom. The only promotion she wanted to hear about was one that involved putting a "Mrs." in front of her name. Or the title "Mother of" after it.

Infertility clinic, my foot, she thought, taking a giant swig of wine. She already knew her ovaries worked. The proof was in the box under her bed.

Speaking of ovaries…shouldn't she be getting her period about now? Becky reached for her phone and fired up her period-tracking app. Yep. Her last one had been the week before AdWorld. That meant Aunt Flow should show up…

Damn. It should have come a week and a half ago.

Becky's mind froze.

There were all kinds of reasons why she could be late. She'd been under a huge amount of stress. Not sleeping well. Eating too much fast food and drinking too much wine.

But being stressed out was a way of life for her. And she didn't eat all that well on even the best of days.

And she had been having lots of sex. But they'd been safe about it, right? She thought hard, trying to remember all the moments they'd stopped to put a condom on. Yep. They had. Every single time. Except…

The afternoon of the sword fight.

Neither of them had even thought about a condom. She hadn't even realized they'd forgotten until she'd seen the undeniable evidence in her underwear while getting into her pajamas that evening.

She raced to the bathroom and tore off her shirt and bra. If she wasn't mistaken her boobs did look bigger than usual. She squeezed one, just to see.

"Ow!"

Yep. They were tender.

Time to call in the troops.

She pulled out her phone and texted Jessie.

We have a 911 situation over here.

Seconds later, the phone rang.

"Becky, what's wrong? Are you hurt? Is someone dead?" Jessie asked, sounding breathless and shaken.

"No. Sorry. I didn't mean to scare you."

"Then what was the 911 about?"

"I think I might be pregnant," she said quietly.

"What? How? I mean I know how, but…"

"I'll explain later. Could you come over, please?" Becky asked, hating the tremor in her voice.

Jessie sighed. "I'm kind of on a date."

"Oh. Okay. Never mind. I'll just run out and get a test."

"Keep me posted, okay?"

"I will," she whispered, and hung up.

Knowing she should head right to the drugstore, she instead found herself on her knees in front of her bed, gazing at the old sonogram picture.

How many times had she sworn she'd never put herself in this position again? That she'd protect herself at all costs?

Too many to count.

The first time had been in Pence's office, right after she'd told him she was quitting.

"What do you mean, you quit?" he'd said. "You can't quit."

"Yes, I can. I am. And I'm using my vacation time as my notice. I've got two weeks coming to me," she'd said, hoping beyond hope he couldn't see her knees trembling.

"What will you do?" he'd asked, his voice suddenly cold. "You know as well as I do that I'm the only reason you've made it as far as you have."

"That's not true," she'd said quietly.

"Sure it is. I could've gotten rid of you after your internship was over. But I kept you around. Made sure you got put on the best assignments," he'd said, walking over to his awards shelf. "The only reason you got your award was because I convinced the client to go with your idea."

"They would have chosen it even if you hadn't pushed it," she'd said, anger sparking in her veins. "But you had to feel like you were in control of every part of my life. You never let me do things on my own!"

"That's because you would have failed," he'd said, stalking silently across the plush green carpet toward her. "You screw everything up. Heck, you can't even manage to take your birth control pills the right way."

She'd gasped, his barbed comment tearing open the thin scab on her heart. "Oh, my God, you're unbelievable."

He'd smiled coldly as he came to stand in front of her. "I deserved that, so I won't hold it against you." Then, taking a deep breath, he'd said, "Let's start over. Becky, please don't leave. We've got a good thing going here. Stick with me and you'll be a star."

"I already am a star, Pence. And I don't need you to continue being one."

"No one will hire you," he'd said softly.

"I already have a job," she'd said defiantly.

"Where? Ads R Us?"

"At an agency with more awards than you can count. In a place where they've never heard of you."

"You'll fail," he'd said, turning his back on her.

"No. I won't. I'll knock their socks off," she'd said with more confidence than she'd felt. "But I do have you to thank for one thing."

"What?" he'd said over his shoulder.

"Now I know better than to let some egotistical man get in my head. Or my bed. No one will ever be able to mess up my life the way you have, Pence."

He'd snorted.

"You'll be knocked up and out of the game before the year is up."

"I doubt it. But you'll definitely still be a bitter asshole stuck in a loveless marriage. If she doesn't wise up and leave you."

His answer had been a wordless roar. One she still occasionally heard in her dreams.

Her reverie was broken by a loud buzzing sound. Someone was at the front door.

She got up and shuffled to the intercom. "Hello?"

"Let me in, girl. It's cold out here," Jessie's voice called.

'What happened to your date?"

"You're more important. Now, hit the dang buzzer!"

Becky did, and went to hold the door open for her friend. Jessie bounded up the stairs, plastic bag in hand.

"I come bearing gifts," she said. "Five flavors of pee sticks and two flavors of ice cream."

"I told you I was going to take care of it," Becky protested.

"And did you?"

Becky shook her head.

"Right, then. Pick your poison. Pink, purple, blue, red or generic?" Jessie said, holding the bag out in front of her.

Becky closed her eyes and reached inside.

"Looks like we're going with pink," she said.

Becky sat on the closed toilet lid, eyes squeezed tightly shut. In three minutes she'd have her answer.

There was a soft knock and Jessie came in, her sequined skirt sparkling in the harsh fluorescent light.

"How are you doing?" she asked.

"Well, I won a two-hundred-and-fifty-million-dollar piece of business, told off my ex, got promoted and found out I might be pregnant. All in one day. How could I be anything less than fabulous?" she said.

Jessie squeezed her hand. "It'll be okay," she said.

Her phone alarm shrilled loudly. Becky blew out a big breath of air.

"Do you want to look or do you want me to?" Jessie asked.

"I'll do it," Becky said.

Reaching out with one shaking hand, she grabbed the pink-capped stick from where it sat on the edge of her ugly green tub and looked down.

"Well?" Jessie asked, her voice shaking.

Mutely, Becky held it out for her to see, stomach roiling.

"Oh, no," she breathed. "Becky, I'm sorry."

She was pregnant.

Becky slammed the toilet lid open seconds before her dinner made a reappearance.

"Well," Jessie said, when the heaving had stopped. "That's not the reaction you see on TV."

Becky tried to smile. "Yep, but—as we well know—advertising tells only a selective version of the truth."

Jessie helped her up. "You took the words right out of

my mouth. Now, come on, let's get you out of here. Nothing good comes of extended visits to the bathroom."

A short while later Becky was again stretched out on her purple chaise, a bottle of hastily purchased ginger ale fizzing on the table beside her. Jessie was curled up on her only other piece of furniture—a very faded red couch.

Jessie looked at Becky over the rim of her wine glass. "So, I'm assuming this is Mark's kid, right?"

Becky raised an eyebrow at her. "While I admit my behavior has been a little more reckless than usual, I assure you I haven't been having sex with random men I meet on the street."

"No. I know, I didn't mean… I'm sorry, Becky."

She waved her comment away. "No worries. I understand."

"You know, there's a clinic in my neighborhood. They have a reputation for being very discreet…"

Becky shook her head. "I don't need a clinic. I'm keeping it."

Jessie's jaw dropped.

"Are you sure that's a good idea? I mean, you just got the world's biggest promotion today."

"Positive. I'll figure out how to make it work." She'd made her decision the second she'd seen the plus sign on the pregnancy test. It was the only thing she could do.

Jessie looked unconvinced. "Well, if you change your mind, just let me know. I'd be happy to go with you."

Suddenly angry, Becky glared at her friend. "How could you say that to me? You know what happened…before. Having that abortion almost destroyed me. Do you want me to have to go through that again?"

Jessie paled. "I'm sorry. I…I wasn't thinking. I just don't want you to rush into anything. It's a big decision."

Becky immediately regretted her outburst. Her friend

had never been anything but supportive. And there was no way she could know how concrete her decision was.

"I'm sorry, Jessie. You didn't deserve that. But I'm keeping this baby. I couldn't live with any other choice."

Jessie nodded. "All right. Well, I'll support you, then."

Becky smiled her thanks and the two women sat silently for a while. Becky thanked her lucky stars she'd gotten that bonus check today. She'd be able to buy the baby everything it needed. And, she thought, looking around her shoebox-size apartment, she might even be able to afford a bigger place.

"What are you going to do about Mark?" Jessie asked suddenly.

Her brain stuttered. "Do?"

"Well, you're going to have to tell him. It's not like he won't notice. Besides, he deserves to know."

Unbelievably, she'd forgotten about that small detail. She'd been thinking about the baby as hers, not theirs.

"You're right," she said. "I don't think he's going to be very happy though. He's pretty anti-kids."

"Well," Jessie said, "whatever happens, you know I'll be there for you. I'll even be your labor coach, if you want."

Becky laughed. "I'm not quite ready to think about that yet."

Jessie looked at her watch, then heaved herself off of the couch. "Man, it's getting late. I better get going so you can get some rest. Are you going to be okay?"

Becky nodded.

"Okay," she said, wrapping her rainbow scarf around her neck. "Take care of yourself."

"I will."

After one final hug Jessie was gone.

Becky sank to the floor and hugged her knees, allowing herself to hope for a minute. Mark had been ready to start a relationship this afternoon. Maybe it would all be okay.

Her mind flashed back to the way he'd behaved with that little boy on the way to the park. He was a natural. Maybe he'd jump at the chance to be a dad.

And maybe pigs were getting ready to fly.

Oh, well. No time like the present to get the ball rolling.

Pulling out her phone, she texted Mark.

We need to talk.

Almost instantly her phone pinged with his reply.

I'm listening, Gorgeous Girl.

Not over text. In person. Dinner tomorrow?

Sure. Where?

Come over. I'll cook.

This was a conversation that needed to be held in private.

See you at seven?

Can't wait.

A bald-faced lie.

Hopefully tomorrow night would go better than it had the last time she'd had this conversation with a man.

It could hardly be worse.

CHAPTER TEN

MARK WOKE UP on Saturday morning feeling happier than he could remember ever being. For once, all was right with his world.

He swung his legs over the edge of the bed and padded across the hardwood floor of his studio apartment to the granite kitchen island where the fifty-thousand-dollar check was sitting. He ran his finger across the dollar amount. All those zeroes belonged to him. And he hadn't had to beg his stepfather for a penny of it.

On impulse, he snapped a picture of the check and texted his mother.

Your boy done good. Got promoted to creative director yesterday. With this as a bonus.

He hit Send and waited for a response. None came.

Not that he had really expected anything else. His mother had made it quite clear over the years that she'd really rather her son disappeared so she could focus on the family she *did* want.

Shake it off, he told himself. Much better to focus on the things he had a chance of fixing—like his relationship with Becky.

And, although it scared him to admit it, he did want a relationship. He wanted to wander the city with her. He wanted to walk in Little Italy at night and explore Central Park during the day. He wanted to eat with her in her tiny apartment and see her golden hair spread out on his pillows after a night of love.

Not even the fact that they worked together deterred him. They made a crazy good team—both in and out of the office.

All he had to do was convince her to give it a try.

Night had already descended when Mark arrived on Becky's doorstep, bearing a bottle of wine and a bunch of daisies tied with a ribbon that matched her eyes.

Taking a deep breath, he pushed the buzzer.

Seconds later, the door clicked open.

Becky was waiting for him at the top of the dark staircase. "Hey, Magic Man," she said with a smile.

"Hey, yourself," he said, taking the time to appreciate the plunging blue V-neck top and tight black leather skirt she was wearing. "You're looking even more gorgeous than usual, Gorgeous Girl."

"Thank you," she said shyly, turning her cheek when he reached down to kiss her.

Hmm. That was a new one.

He handed her the wine and flowers. "For my beautiful hostess," he said.

"How did you know daisies were my favorite?" she asked.

"Lucky guess," he said.

She ushered him inside, then busied herself in the kitchen, putting the flowers in water. "Make yourself at home," she called.

While small, her apartment felt cozy and warm. The walls were painted a cheerful yellow and decorated with pictures of brightly colored flowers and tropical beaches. Although a tiny dining table was tucked away in one corner, a giant purple chaise dominated the room. It shared the space with a comfortable-looking couch and a plethora of rainbow-hued pillows.

"I don't think I mentioned it the last time I was here, but I really love your place."

"Thank you," she said, rounding the corner from the kitchen. "It's tiny, but I kind of love it."

"From what I can tell, every apartment in New York is tiny—even the ones you pay millions of dollars for."

"That's true," she said. "Although I hear the roaches in the expensive ones wear diamond-plated shells."

"That figures. Roaches are excellent at adapting to their surroundings."

She laughed and reached up to kiss him. "Thank you for coming," she whispered.

When he sensed her backing away, he reached out to pull her closer.

"I wouldn't have missed this for the world," he said. "Maybe later we can have dessert in bed again. This time I'll be the plate."

"Mmm," she said with an enigmatic smile. "We'll see how the evening goes. Are you hungry?"

"Starving."

"Good. I've got lasagna. It'll be ready in just a sec."

"Can I help?"

"No need. Unless you want to open the wine?"

He followed her into the kitchen and took the bottle she handed him.

"Glasses are on the table," she said. "But just pour me a drop."

"Are you sure? The guy at the wine shop told me this was an excellent vintage—whatever that means."

"I'm sure," she said.

She was definitely acting a little odd. He hoped it was because she was trying to get used to the idea of them being a couple and not because she had something bad to tell him.

Mentally he shook his head. No use borrowing trouble before he had it.

Soon Becky brought out plates of lasagna and garlic bread.

“It looks awesome,” he said.

“I hope so,” she said. “Dig in!”

He picked up his wine glass. “I’d like to propose a toast,” he said.

Becky smiled and raised her glass. “Okay, let’s hear it.”

“To the kick-ass team that is us. Here’s hoping this is the beginning of a long and beautiful relationship.”

She seemed to wince a little at his words, but gamely clinked her glass with his. “To us,” she murmured.

An awkward silence fell, and Mark watched as Becky picked at her food.

He let the quiet go on, hoping she’d be the one to break it. She didn’t.

“Becky, what’s wrong?”

She looked up, her eyes bright with unshed tears.

“I have something to tell you,” she said. “Something I’m pretty sure you’re not going to like.”

Trying not to be alarmed, he said, “Try me.”

She took a deep breath. “There’s no easy way to say this,” she said. “So I’m just going to blurt it out.”

“Okay. You’re not dying or married or something, are you?”

“No. Nothing like that. I’m just pregnant.”

He heard a distant clatter as his fork dropped from his suddenly nerveless fingers.

“I’m sorry. I think I misheard you. You’re what?”

“Pregnant.” She made herself say it again. “I’m pregnant. With your baby.”

“What? How can that be?” he spluttered.

“Well, you see, there’s this stork,” she said, trying for

humor. "Last night he flew by my window and told me he'd be delivering a baby to us in about eight months. I told him he was mistaken, but he showed me the paperwork. It was all in order."

"This is no time for jokes," Mark snapped. "I don't understand. We used protection."

"We did. All except for one time."

She could see his mind working busily, trying to connect the dots.

"What? When?"

"Remember the afternoon of the sword fight?"

He paled as she watched.

"Son of a..." Mark swore. "I can't believe we were so stupid. *Damn it!*"

He put his head in his hands. After a moment, he took a deep breath.

"Okay. You're pregnant. It happens. Unplanned pregnancies happen all the time. But we can fix this."

He got up and started to pace.

"How far along are you?"

"Just five or six weeks."

"Oh. Good. That's not very far at all. You can probably even still get that pill from your doctor. The one that causes a miscarriage or whatever."

"Mark?"

He stopped and looked at her. "What?"

"I don't want to do that."

"Okay, well, there's bound to be a good clinic around here somewhere. It is New York, after all."

"No," she said. "I don't want an abortion."

He looked sick—as if she had just punched him in the stomach.

"What are you saying?"

"I want to keep it," she said quietly. Then, with more determination, "I'm *going* to keep it. I want this baby, Mark."

"No. You don't."

"Yes," she said, getting annoyed, "I do. I'm a grown woman, Mark. I know what I'm doing."

"No, you don't!" he said, his face turning red. "You only think you do. But once he's born he'll get in the way. There will be sick days and doctor visits and daycare issues. You'll be exhausted all the time, and frazzled, and run down. Before you know it your career will be in the tank. Soon, you'll start to resent him for being born. You'll wish you'd gotten rid of him while you still could. No kid deserves to go through life like that, Becky. No kid should be stuck with a mother who doesn't want him around."

He gazed down at her, shoulders hunched, and she could see a lifetime of hurt reflected in his eyes.

"Please don't do this, Becky."

Becky's heart broke for the man in front of her, and for the mother who obviously hadn't been able to give him what he needed.

She went to him, cupping his cheek gently with her hand.

"It won't be like that, Mark. I've only known about this baby for twenty-four hours and I already love him with all my heart. I always will."

"You can't promise that, Becky," he said miserably. "You don't know what it's like. How hard it is."

"I won't be alone. I'll be surrounded by people who love me—and him. Heck, my mother will probably try to move in with me. The only question is whether you're going to be one of those people."

"What are you asking me, Becky?"

She pulled him down on the couch next to her. "Yesterday you were begging me to give this relationship a chance. To give us a shot. Now I'm asking you the same thing."

Grabbing his hand, she placed it over her stomach.

"Are you willing to see if we can make this work? To

give this family a shot? The stakes are a lot higher now, but I'm willing to go all-in if you are."

He looked at her with horror on his face.

"Are you asking me to *marry* you?"

She snorted. "As if. No. I'm just asking you not to slam the door shut. To be a part of our lives. To see if you can make room for this baby in your heart."

His face grew cold and he stood.

"No, Becky. I'm sorry, but I can't. If you want this baby it's all on you. I won't be a part of it."

She nodded and swallowed, looking down at her hands so he wouldn't see the tears in her eyes.

"Okay. I understand."

A moment later she heard the door open and shut. She was alone.

She rubbed her stomach absently. "Looks like it's just you and me, kid," she whispered, tears running down her face.

Funny. Yesterday she hadn't been sure she wanted to let Mark into her heart. It was only now that he was gone that she realized she already had. And that when he'd left he'd taken half of it with him.

Mark stomped down the cold dark streets, glaring at anyone who dared to meet his eye.

How could she have let this happen? He had assumed she was on some kind of birth control. That she was behaving like a responsible adult.

It wasn't fair. Just when he'd thought he'd finally found a place where he could make a career he was stuck working with a woman who wanted more from him than he could give. A woman who was pregnant with his baby, for God's sake.

The sound of his phone ringing yanked Mark into the

present. Fishing it out of his pocket, he looked at his screen. It was his mother. Impeccable timing, as always.

He considered flinging his phone into the street, but decided talking to her would probably give him all the confirmation he needed that he was making the right decision.

"Hello, Mother."

"Mark, darling, I got your text. How wonderful!"

"I sent that twelve hours ago," he snarled.

"Yes, I know. But we had a tennis tournament today at the club. And then the Petersons came over for dinner. They send their love, by the way."

"Do the Petersons even know who I am?"

"Of course they do, Mark. They've been coming to the house since you were in the seventh grade."

"Yes, but I was never there," he said.

"Oh, don't be so dramatic. You were home for nearly every school vacation. For months at a time in the summer, in fact."

"Only if you couldn't find somewhere else to send me," he said.

There was a beat of silence. "What is this all about, Mark? I made sure you had the best education money could buy. Was that wrong?"

"Oh, come on, Mom. I know the only reason you sent me to boarding school was because you couldn't stand to have me around. Didn't want to be reminded of your mistakes after you married into money. I didn't belong in your fancy new family."

"Is that what you thought?" his mother said, her voice a horrified whisper. "Mark, you couldn't be more wrong. Why, I—"

"Save it for someone who cares, Mom. I gave up a long time ago."

It wasn't until he hung up that he realized he'd been

shouting. Good thing he was in New York. Nothing fazed the people here.

God, he needed a drink. A stiff one. Looking up, he realized he was standing right across the street from a bar.

He'd get drunk tonight. Then decide what to do about the train wreck that was his life in the morning.

CHAPTER ELEVEN

BY THE TIME Monday morning dawned Becky had bottled up her heartbreak and shoved it into the darkest recesses of her brain. She couldn't afford to be weak.

She was starting a new job: working with a man who would prefer never to see her again and for a man who still had a hard time believing she was anything but a pretty face.

She was going to have to be on her A-game every day from here on out. She'd have to prove she was worth every dime they were paying her and, pregnant or not, could kick the ass of every male creative in the city.

That was the only way she'd be able to get through this with both her pride and career intact.

She spent the entire train ride pumping herself up. By the time she strode through SBD's doors she had convinced herself that she could handle absolutely anything the world cared to throw at her. Even a lifetime of working with Mark.

But she couldn't bite back the sigh of relief that came when she realized she had beaten him to the office. With luck, she could have her stuff packed up and moved into her new space before he arrived.

Becky grabbed a box and got to work. She hadn't gotten very far, though, when there was a knock on the door.

"Come in," she called.

David's executive assistant glided through the door.

"Hi, Pam, what can I do for you?"

"I take it you didn't see the email I sent you?" the elegant woman asked.

"No," she answered slowly. "Is something wrong?"

"I don't think so," she said, looking everywhere but at Becky. "But David did say he wanted to see you as soon as you got in."

"All right," Becky said. "Then I guess I'll head up there with you now."

The two women spent the elevator ride in an increasingly heavy silence. Becky was practically squirming by the time they arrived on the forty-third floor.

"I'll let him know you're here," Pam said. "Why don't you have a seat?"

Sensing it was more of a command than a request, Becky sat down in one of the black leather chairs.

She wished she had some idea of what this was all about. Mark wouldn't have told David about her pregnancy… would he?

Thankfully Pam returned before that train of thought could go any further.

"You can go in now," she said.

Becky thanked her and squared her shoulders before stepping through the heavy oak door.

David was ensconced behind his giant mahogany desk, his chair arranged on a riser so he could tower over the people sitting in front of him. But he wasn't alone.

Mark sat in one of the chestnut-colored club chairs while Cindy, the head of HR, perched on the couch.

No one looked happy.

"Ah, there you are, Becky," David boomed. "I was beginning to think we were going to have to send a search party after you."

"Sorry," she said. "I was downstairs. I just hadn't opened my email yet."

'Not to worry," he said. "We've been having a nice little chat while we waited—haven't we, Mark?"

Mark nodded, his face looking pale and strained.

"Good, I'm glad I haven't inconvenienced anyone. May I ask why we're all here?"

David nodded. "I'm going to cut right to the chase, Becky. It's come to my attention that you and Mark are involved in a relationship."

"Excuse me? We most definitely are *not,*" she said sharply.

"Don't try to deny it, dear. I have security camera footage of the two of you engaged in rather passionate embraces in several places throughout the building."

Oh, no.

"Yes, well, that may be true, but I can assure you that any relationship we may have had has already come to an end. Tell him, Mark!"

Mark glowered at her. "I already tried."

"Be that as it may, I am afraid you two are in blatant violation of your contracts with us. Cindy, could you read the relevant clause to them?"

The woman nodded. "It's in section twenty-seven A on page seventeen," she said. "'The employee agrees to refrain from establishing relationships of a romantic or sexual nature with any SBD employee, vendor, client, or contractor. If conduct of this nature is discovered the employee understands that he or she will be considered to have violated his or her contract, and will be subject to punitive action up to and including termination of employment.'"

Becky paled. "I honestly don't remember seeing that in my contract," she said.

"It was there," Cindy said. "I have your initialed copy right here. I suggest you pay closer attention to what you're signing in the future."

She nodded, furiously trying to process the predicament she now found herself in. "Obviously. So where does that leave us, David?"

He took a deep breath and smiled a nasty smile.

"If this was an ordinary situation I would dismiss both of you and wash my hands of the whole thing. But it isn't. As you know, Eden has specifically requested that you both be on their team. Which was why I promoted the two of you to the codirector positions. However, in light of this new information, I cannot, in good conscience, allow that arrangement to stand. Therefore I am going to allow one of you to stay and continue on in a creative director capacity. The other person will be allowed to resign, with the bonus received on Friday serving as a severance package. I'm leaving it to you to decide who will go and who will stay. You have until the end of the day."

Becky blinked. *They* had to decide who got fired? Who *did* that?

"But what about Eden? They want both of us on their team," she blurted.

"I'll tell Eden that whichever one of you resigns has had a family emergency and will be on leave indefinitely, and that you'll return to work on their account when things are squared away. You won't, of course, but by the time they figure that out they'll have forgotten why they thought they needed you both anyway. That's it. You're dismissed," David finished. "Now, get out of my sight."

She didn't have to be told twice. She was punching the elevator button before Mark had even risen from his chair.

Unfortunately the elevator was its usual poky self. By the time the door dinged open Mark was approaching. She stepped in and held the door, unable to abandon her innate Midwestern politeness even in a time of crisis.

"Thanks," Mark muttered.

She nodded.

"Look," he said, "I know we need to talk about this, but—"

"I can't right now," Becky cut in. "I need time to wrap my brain around everything we just heard."

There was an awkward pause as Mark stared at the ceiling.

"I guess I was wrong. Someone did watch that footage of us in the elevator," he said.

"Whoever it was certainly got an eyeful."

"You don't think David saw it, do you?" Becky asked with a dawning sense of horror.

"Oh, I'm sure he did. The man is a horndog, you know."

The elevator dinged again and they arrived at their floor.

"Look, I'm going to go for a walk and try to sort things out," Mark said. "How about we meet for a late lunch?"

"Sure. The halal cart at one-thirty?"

"You got it," he said, and headed off.

Becky knocked on Jessie's office door.

"Come in," she called.

"It still feels weird not to be sitting here anymore," Becky said as she entered.

"You're welcome in my closet anytime," Jessie said. "Your chair is still here and everything."

"Thanks," Becky said. "But I don't think I'm going to be working here very much longer."

"What are you talking about? You're my new boss, aren't you?"

"It's a long story. Let's go get some coffee."

Once they were settled in their favorite booth, with steaming cups of coffee, Becky launched into the story.

"So one of you has to quit?"

"That's the long and the short of it."

"Well, obviously it should be Mark. You're the one who belongs here. He just got hired!"

Becky sighed. "That would make the most sense, I know."

"But..."

"But I think I'm just going to do it. David will never

respect me now that he's seen me in such a compromised position, and I'm tired of fighting to prove myself to him."

"What about your promotion?"

"I don't know. It doesn't seem so important anymore." As soon as she said the words Becky realized she meant them. Although she'd been prepared to fight to keep her job, her heart wasn't in it. It was still lying in pieces on the floor of her apartment.

"It sounds like you've already made up your mind," Jessie said.

Becky sipped her decaffeinated coffee in silence for a moment. Truth was, she'd known in her gut what she needed to do almost before the words had come out of David's mouth.

"Yes," she said finally. "I guess I have."

"I sure am going to miss you," Jessie said sadly.

Becky reached across the table to squeeze her hand. "Don't worry. You're still going to see me. You volunteered to be my birth coach, remember?"

"Oh, yeah. I forgot about that. Cool!"

Taking a deep breath, Becky prepared to launch into the real reason she'd asked Jessie to have coffee with her. "So, listen, I need you to do me a favor."

"Anything."

Mark sat on a bench in front of the halal cart, waiting for Becky.

He'd racked his brain for a good solution all morning, but still didn't know what to do.

Common sense dictated that he be the one to go. After all, Becky had been working for years to get the promotion they'd just been granted. He'd just stepped in.

But he wanted to stay. He wanted to launch the Eden campaign into the stratosphere and make a name for himself. He wanted to earn a steady paycheck, get to know his colleagues, just live like a normal human being for a while.

But Becky was pregnant. She needed this job and the medical insurance that came with it. He might not want the baby, but that didn't mean he wanted the child to be denied basic medical care.

He sighed, hating the fact that at his core he still seemed to be a decent human being. Life would be easier if he could stop caring about other people.

He knew he had to be the one to walk away. He couldn't live with himself otherwise.

"Hi, handsome," a voice said from beside him.

He jumped. "Where did you come from, Jessie?" he said to the woman who had suddenly appeared next to him.

"I've been sitting here for five minutes. You've just been on another planet," she said.

"All right, then, here's a better question. What are you doing here?"

"Becky sent me," she said. "She asked me to give you this."

In her hand was a bright blue envelope. It looked like a greeting card.

"You're to read it, then ask me your questions."

"Okay," he said, hoping he sounded calmer than he felt. What could this be about?

Taking a deep breath, he opened the envelope and pulled out the card. The outside featured a black-and-white image of a magician. The inside was cramped with Becky's writing.

Dear Magic Man,

By the time you read this I will have already submitted my resignation. The job is yours. Enjoy it. Rest assured, though, that I will be watching you. If you don't turn our concept into a showstopping, award-eating monster, I'm going to come back and kick your ass.

Please don't try to get in touch. Don't call. Don't email. Don't stop by. I don't want to ever see you again. At least not until you're ready to step up and be a dad. Which, let's be honest, will probably never happen.

So this is goodbye. Have a nice life, Mark. You deserve to be happy.

Your Gorgeous Girl

XOXO

P.S. Jessie will know how to find me. Just in case you ever want to know.

Mark read the note three times. Finally, he looked up. "So, she's gone?"

"Well, not yet. But she's leaving."

"Where is she going?"

"Come on, Mark. You know I can't tell you that."

"Do you know why she's leaving?"

"I'm going to guess it's got something to do with the little seed you planted in her belly," Jessie said, rolling her eyes.

"Hey, that wasn't my fault," he said.

"Whatever, dude. It takes two to tango."

She had him there.

"Right. Well, I'll see you back at the office," she said, hopping up off the bench. "Enjoy your lunch."

After she left Mark waited for the relief to set in. After all, Becky had given him what he wanted. He'd be able to keep his dream job for as long as he wanted.

He should be happy. Instead he was miserable.

She hadn't even left yet, and he already missed her.

That couldn't be a good sign.

CHAPTER TWELVE

BECKY SAT ON the bed in her childhood room, trying to find the energy to unpack. It had been an exhausting week. She'd whirled into action the very same day that she'd quit, burying her pain in activity.

Finding a renter to sublet her apartment and getting her things packed had been the easy part. Making peace with leaving New York had been a good deal harder. She'd always thought she'd spend the rest of her life there. She'd dreamed of having a wedding in Central Park and of raising a family in a brownstone on the Upper West Side. And as for her career—well, she'd assumed she'd spend it in the ad agencies on Madison Avenue.

Returning home to Michigan had never been part of the plan.

But without a job she didn't have a lot of choices. Her fifty thousand dollars wouldn't last very long in New York. And raising a baby alone in the city was a challenge she wasn't sure she was up for.

So here she was, back where she'd started. She sniffed, quiet tears falling down her face. So much for her big plans.

There was a soft knock on the door.

"Come in," she said, hastily wiping the evidence away.

Her mother entered, carrying a laundry basket.

"I brought you some clean sheets."

"Th-thanks, Mom."

"Are you crying?'

"No. Yes. Maybe?"

"Oh, honey," her mother said, perching on the bed beside her. "I know things look bad right now. But it'll get better. Before you know it you'll have a job, and a place of your own, and a baby to love."

"I never meant for this to happen, Mom," she said, leaning her head on her mother's shoulder. "I'm sorry if I've disappointed you."

"You could never disappoint me," she said. "Especially not when you're carrying my grandchild! It would have been better if you'd gotten yourself a husband first, of course. But you're young. It will happen in its own good time."

Becky looked at her mom, flabbergasted. That didn't sound like the conservative Catholic she knew her to be. "I didn't expect you to be so calm about all of this," she said.

"We've been watching a lot of reality TV these last few years," she said. "I know the world has changed."

Becky just barely managed to stop herself from laughing. She could tell her mother was completely serious.

"Well, I appreciate it. You don't know how much."

"Not to worry. It's all part of the job. You'll find out soon enough."

Becky put her hand on her still-flat belly.

"I guess I will at that." The thought filled her with fear. "Mom?"

"What, honey?"

"Do you think I'll be any good at it? At being a mother?"

"Of course you will. You'll be an amazing mother."

"But I don't even like kids."

Her mother laughed out loud. "You probably never will like other people's children. But you'll always love your own. Trust me."

Since she didn't have many choices, Becky decided to try.

Mark scowled as he examined the printout Jessie had brought him.

"Jessie, this is nothing like we discussed," he said.

"I know, but I thought this was better," she said. "No offense, but your idea kind of sucked."

"Jessie, I'm your boss. You can't talk to me like that," he snapped.

"Just look at it," she said. "Please?"

"No. I need you to do what I asked you to do. *Now.*"

She glared at him and stomped out.

Sighing, he sat down in his chair and glanced at the printout. He hated to admit it, but she was right. It *was* better.

He called to his assistant. "Susan?"

She poked her head in the door, looking tense. "Yes, Mark?"

"Can you ask Jessie to come back to my office, please?"

She nodded and left.

A few minutes later Jessie returned, looking even more furious than she had when she'd left.

"You wanted to see me?"

"Yes. Sit."

She did—reluctantly.

"Look, I'm sorry," he said. "This *is* better. I don't know what the hell is wrong with me lately."

Jessie snorted. "I do. Its name is Becky."

"This has nothing to do with Becky," he said, feeling the weight of the lie in his heart.

"Whatever you say, dude. Have you told the client she's gone yet?"

"We've told them she's taking a leave of absence. We didn't clue them in to the fact that it's a permanent one." And if he had his way they wouldn't. At least not until they were happy with what he and his team had put together without her. He owed it to Becky to keep them on board and in love.

"I could dress up in a blond wig and pretend to be her at your next meeting if you want."

He laughed. "Thanks for the offer, but I don't think that would go over very well."

"Okay, but if you get desperate you know where to find me," she said, turning to go.

"Hey, Jessie?" he asked, hating himself for what he was about to say.

"Yeah?"

"Have you heard from her?"

"Her who?"

"You know who. Becky."

"Oh, her. Yeah. She's okay…considering."

His blood ran cold. He'd never forgive himself if something bad had happened to her… "Considering what? Is something wrong?"

"She's pregnant. Unemployed. And the father's being a dumbass. So, yeah. There are some things that are wrong."

He had asked for that, he guessed. Sighing, he motioned for her to go, but she was already gone.

He'd thought it would be easy to forget about Becky. After all, their—well, whatever it was they'd shared had only lasted a few weeks. Just the blink of an eye, all things considered.

But he missed her right down to his core. He'd thought about asking Jessie to give him her contact information on a hundred different occasions, but stopped himself every time. No matter how much he wanted Becky, he did not want to be a father to their child. Which meant he had to respect her wishes and stay away.

Just as he was about to sink into a vat of self pity there was a knock on his door.

"Yeah—come in," he said.

"That's how you greet your guests?" a familiar voice asked. "I thought I had taught you better than that."

Mark looked up and was shocked to see his mother

standing there, looking out of place in her conservative pantsuit and sensible shoes.

"Mom? What are you doing here?" he said, trying not to let the shock show as he rounded his desk to give her a hug.

"Oh, you know. I was in the neighborhood and thought I'd stop by."

"Mom, you live in Connecticut."

"I just came into the city to do some shopping," she said, picking nonexistent dust off her navy jacket.

"You hate shopping in New York," he said, flabbergasted.

"All right," she said. "I came specifically to see you, if you must know."

"Why?" She'd never done that. *Ever.*

"Because I haven't heard from you since that night you yelled at me over the phone. I was worried."

Worried? His mom was worried about him? That was news to him. He couldn't stop the sudden warming of his heart.

"You could have called."

"I did. Repeatedly. You never answered."

Damn it. She had him there. He was behaving more like a spoiled teenager than the adult he was.

"Look, Mom, I'm sorry. Let's start over, okay? It's lovely to see you."

"Thank you, Mark. It's wonderful to see you, too. Do you have time for lunch?"

He really didn't, but he'd have to be a total ass to tell her so.

"Sure. Where would you like to go?"

"I've already booked a table, darling. The car's waiting downstairs."

She had chosen a kitschy bistro in Little Italy, complete with red-checkered tablecloths and traditional Italian music playing in the background.

"This has always been one of my favorites, but your stepfather won't come here," she told him as she settled herself into her seat. "The lasagna is to die for, but he can't appreciate it. Too many carbs, he says. As if that's possible."

"He does seem to have a hard time appreciating anything enjoyable," Mark said blandly.

"He means well—you know that. But he takes his responsibilities very seriously. He has a hard time letting go."

"That's the understatement of the year."

"Be nice, Mark," his mother said sharply.

"Sorry," he said. But he wasn't. Not really.

A smiling waiter came to greet them. "Lucille," he said. "How lovely to see you. The usual?"

"Yes, please." She smiled.

Turning to Mark, he said, "And you, sir?"

"I'm told the lasagna is to die for. So I guess I'll try that. In fact, bring me whatever she's having."

"Very well. Two usuals. I took the liberty of bringing your favorite wine with me, Lucille. Would you like me to pour?"

"Certainly. Mark, can you have a glass during working hours?"

"Sure, why not?" He'd probably need it to get through this conversation.

Once the waiter had retreated his mother looked at him with a serious expression on her face.

"I want to talk about our last conversation," she said.

"Look, Mom, I was out of line. I'm sorry. We don't need to talk about it."

"Yes. We do," she said, a hint of steel in her voice. "We need to clear the air. Or at least I do. Now, listen very closely. I love you very much. I always have. I sent you away to school because your stepfather insisted it was necessary to ensure you had the best possible foundation for college. Every family we know did the same thing. It's what people with money do."

Mark squirmed uncomfortably. He so didn't want to have this conversation.

"It felt like he was just trying to get me out of the way. Why would he want to look at his wife's illegitimate child every day if he didn't have to? Especially since everyone knew I was a mistake."

"You probably won't believe me when I tell you this, but he's very proud of you."

"That's not what you said when I was a kid. You told me I was an embarrassment to you both almost every time you saw me," he said, unable to keep the whine from his voice.

"I admit when you got yourself thrown out of three boarding schools in the space of one term I was a bit frustrated with you. Anyone would have been. I probably said some things I didn't mean. But, Mark, I never meant to make you feel unwanted. You're one of the best things that ever happened to me—even if you were, ahem, unexpected."

"Did you ever regret having me?" he blurted, unable to stop himself from asking.

"Never. Not even for a minute. How could I? You're my son. I can't imagine life without you," she said, practically glowing with sincerity.

Mark smiled, surprised to realize how much her answer mattered.

"Thank you," he said. "Thank you for telling me that."

Their food arrived and they applied themselves to the delicious baked concoction, watching the traffic go by on the street outside. A mother passed by with a gorgeous little blonde girl in tow. The child saw them looking and waved, her whole face lighting up as she smiled. Mark laughed and waved back.

"I hope you have children of your own someday," his

mother said, a certain wistfulness playing across her face. "A family makes life worth living."

"Maybe someday," Mark said, trying not to think about the baby currently growing in Becky's womb. "When I'm ready."

His mother snorted. "You'll never be ready. No one ever is. You just figure it out as you go along and hope you don't make too many mistakes."

He nodded. He was pretty sure if he told his mom what had happened she'd tell him he'd already made a giant one.

Becky slammed her car door and hit her fist on the steering wheel. This had been the week's third job interview and it had been just as big of a bust as the last two.

Although her interviewer probably didn't think so. Judging from the light in his eyes when they'd said goodbye, he thought he had found his next senior copywriter. If only the job hadn't sounded so boring.

Her phone blared in the silence. She looked down at the number. It was the recruiter she'd been working with.

"Hi, Amy," she said, sighing into the phone.

"Hey, girl, you rocked another one," an excited voice said. "I just talked to Jim and he said he'll have an offer put together by the end of the week. That means you'll have three opportunities to choose from."

"That's nice," Becky said.

"Really? I tell you you're about to have three offers thrown at you and all you can say is 'That's nice'?"

"It's just—well, I don't want to work on cars," she said.

There was a beat of silence. "Becky. You *do* realize you're in Detroit, right? Cars are what we do here."

"I know, I know. And I'll do it. It just doesn't thrill me."

"Well, I'll bet you'll feel differently when the offers come in. They're going to throw buckets of money at you, honey."

"All right. Call me if you hear anything," she said, and hung up the phone.

She turned the key in the ignition and drove out of the soulless office park. Everything here seemed so sterile. Although cars jammed the streets, there was not a single person on the sidewalk. There was no music. No street vendors. Not even any taxis leaning on their horns. It was as if somebody had hit the mute button on the world.

The leaden skies didn't help, either. The only thing worse than early December in Detroit was late February in Detroit. It was cold. Wet. And eternally cloudy. Only the twinkling Christmas lights that winked into life after the sun went down relieved the monotony.

But that didn't help during the day.

God, but she missed Mark…er…New York.

She put her hand on her belly and sighed. "I hope you appreciate what I'm trying to do here, kiddo. Because I gotta tell you, it kind of sucks."

Mark stepped into the dimly lit bar, hoping a night out with his college roommate would snap him out of the funk he'd found himself in. Quickly he scanned the room, looking for the former football player.

It didn't take long to find him. Although John had blown his knee out the season before, he was still the guy who'd kicked the winning field goal in the Super Bowl a couple of years back. He attracted a crowd wherever he went.

Tonight he was surrounded by a gaggle of beautiful women, as usual.

He strode up to the booth and slapped him on the shoulder.

"Hey, Casanova," he said.

Immediately John turned and grinned. "Mark, you made it! Sit down, buddy. It's been too long."

"It has, hasn't it? We'll have to make up for lost time. What are you drinking? I'll get the next round."

John waved his arm dismissively. "Don't worry about it. Unless you've cozied up to that rich stepdad of yours I've got more money than you do. Still like tequila?"

He nodded.

"All right." He motioned to the bartender. "Jake, I'm going to need a double of Patrón. Fast."

Within moments a large glass of tequila landed in front of Mark.

He downed it, trying hard not to think of the last time he'd done shots of tequila—or who he'd done them with.

Unfortunately his brain insisted on showing him Becky's eyes glittering at him from behind an empty shot glass.

Her voice echoed in his ears. *All right. Let's toast,* she'd said, raising her glass. *To one wild night.*

He'd clinked his glass and locked eyes with hers. *To one wild, scandalous night.*

If he'd known how much that one night would change his life he probably would have walked away after that toast. Although he was really glad he hadn't. Even if what they'd had wasn't meant to last, he was glad he'd gotten the chance to experience it. To experience *her.*

"Hey, dude. You still with us?" John asked.

Mark shook his head to clear it. "Yeah, man. Sorry. Just lost in my thoughts."

"Ri—ight. Dude, the last time I saw you looking this pathetic you'd just found out about Sandra… Oh. This is about a chick, isn't it?"

Mark just looked at him. "I don't want to talk about it. Especially not while you're covered in women."

"Say no more," John said. "Okay, ladies, it's time to shove off. I'll see you later, okay?"

Although they pouted and whined they slowly left the booth. Once they were alone, John turned back to him.

"Okay, out with it. What's wrong?"

"Nothing," said Mark, looking down at his newly refilled shot glass. "I'm just a little off my game tonight."

"Right," he said. "And I'm Robert DeNiro. Try again."

He looked at him and sighed. "All right, but you're going to think I'm a jerk."

John just looked him, one eyebrow raised. "I'll be the judge of that."

By the time the story was done the tequila was long gone. John took one last swig of his beer, then shook his head.

"You were right," he said.

"About what?"

"I do think you're a jerk. How could you abandon her like that?"

Immediately he felt his hackles rise. "I didn't abandon her. It was her choice to go. She left without even telling me."

John stood. "Only after you proved yourself to be an immature cad who runs the second the going gets tough. She did the right thing."

"Where are you going?"

"Nowhere. But you're leaving. You've got no business being here, Mark. Man up and go get your woman. You're too old to sulk because things got too real."

Unable to think of anything to say, Mark got up and left. He didn't want to drink with someone who was lecturing him, anyway.

He wasn't sulking. And he certainly wasn't immature. He'd done Becky a favor by refusing to get involved—better that the child never have a father than have one who didn't really love his mom. He knew from experience how much that sucked.

And he didn't love Becky. He was infatuated, maybe, but not in love.

It never would have lasted.

Even if he did love her she wouldn't have stuck around. A woman like that could have any man she wanted. She'd never be happy settling for a schmuck like him.

Logically, he knew he had done the right thing.

Maybe in a couple more years his heart would believe it, too.

Becky lay back on the paper-covered pillow and breathed out, trying to relax. As the technician moved the gel-covered wand around, trying to get a clearer picture, she did her best to avoid thinking about the last time she'd been in this position, or about the baby that first sonogram had shown her.

"There you are, little bean," the technician said. "It's time to check you out."

Becky looked up at the video screen, trying to identify which of the grainy black-and-white blobs was her baby.

"Mmm-hmm," the technician muttered. "That's good. And there's that…perfect." Then, louder, she said, "Ms. Logan, your bean is in good shape. So far everything looks just the way it should."

Becky still wasn't sure where to look. "Good, but can you show me? I'm embarrassed to say I'm not exactly sure what I'm looking at."

"Oh. Of course. Silly me."

She punched a few keys on the computer and in seconds a peanut-shaped fetus zoomed into focus.

"There's your baby," the technician said. "All curled up and ready to grow. Want to hear the heartbeat?"

Becky nodded.

"All right, here it comes!"

Soon a soft, rapid-fire whooshing beat filled the room.

"That…that's my baby?" Becky asked.

She nodded.

"Oh. Oh. wow." She lay silently for a moment, struggling against tears as a flood of emotions washed over her. Joy. Fear. And a fierce, all-consuming wave of love.

She was going to be a mommy. In fact she already was. And this time nothing would stop her from loving her baby with everything she had.

Eventually the technician cleared her throat. "Sorry to rush you, Ms. Logan, but I have another appointment in just a few minutes. I'm going to have to shut this down. How many pictures would you like?"

For a moment she thought about asking for three. One for her, one for her mom, and one to send to Mark. Maybe seeing the baby would bring him around.

But. No. That was just the hormones talking. Mark didn't want to be involved in the baby's life. And she didn't need him to be.

"Just two, please."

Mark was reviewing the latest round of Eden coupon designs when David let himself into his office.

"We're going to the bar. Come with us."

"Oh, I don't know, David. I have a lot of work to do," he said. Truth was, he had no desire to spend a second longer in the older man's company than he had to.

"Come on. I'm tired of seeing you moping around here. It's time to go out and have some fun."

Fun? With David? Somehow, Mark didn't think that was going to happen. But he knew it was important to appear to be a team player.

"All right," he said. "Just let me get my coat."

A short time later he found himself sitting on a stool in David's favorite dive bar.

"Two whiskeys on the rocks," David said to the bartender.

"Actually, I don't—"

"Every ad man drinks whiskey, son. Buck up."

Mark nodded and fell silent. *Think about the money,* he told himself. *And the job. Thanks to this man, you've finally made it. You can drink a little whiskey if it makes him happy.*

When their drinks came David took a deep swallow. Mark copied him, feeling the burn all the way down into his intestines.

"Listen, Mark, I asked you to come for a drink so I could set you straight on a few things," David said.

"Oh?" Why was it everyone wanted to talk to him all of a sudden?

"I know you think what happened to Becky was unfair. That it was none of my business what you two were getting up to once work was done."

"Well, sort of." The man was a master of understatement.

David continued as if he hadn't heard. "Here's the thing, though. It had to be done. If it hadn't been because of you I would have found another reason to get rid of her."

"But she got rid of herself," Mark protested.

"Oh, please. I knew what she would do when I called the two of you in there. I'd even warned the Eden people that she would probably be taking a leave of absence. Becky's got too big of a heart to let someone else take the fall for her. And you have too much common sense to let go of a golden opportunity like this one."

"I'm not sure I follow you," Mark said slowly, his stomach churning.

"Women don't belong in advertising," David said. "Not in the upper ranks, anyway. They're too emotional. Too distracted. Becky is a damn fine copywriter, but she's incapable of achieving the single-minded focus men like you bring to the table. Eventually she would've found a man. Started a family. And just like that her career would have fallen to third place in her priorities. This agency is too important to me to allow it to take anything less than top priority in the lives of my management team. Advertising isn't a business. It's a lifestyle. I have yet to meet a woman who gets that."

He took a sip of his drink and chuckled.

"Sometimes you have to get creative to persuade them to make the right choice. Like, say, with a 'no relationship' clause."

Mark slammed his glass down on the counter, barely containing his sudden fury.

"Wait a minute. Are you're telling me there's *not* a no-relationship clause in our contracts?" he asked.

"There is now," David said with a smug smile.

It was all Mark could do not to punch him.

"Did you actually have proof that Becky and I were involved?"

"Well, I saw you hugging in your office that day. I didn't need any more proof than that. It was written all over your faces."

Mark's jaw dropped. This man was the biggest ass he'd ever met. And he'd chosen him over the woman he loved.

Loved? Yes, *loved.* As soon as the thought ran through his consciousness he could no longer deny the truth. He loved her with every fiber of his being. No job, no matter how awesome, would ever fill the hole her absence had left in his heart.

Suddenly he knew what he had to do. And it didn't involve wasting any more time with the man sitting next to him.

"David, do you have a pen?"

"Sure," he said, reaching into the pocket of his suit coat. "Here you go."

"Thanks," Mark said. Then he grabbed a fresh cocktail napkin from the pile on the bar. Uncapping the pen, he wrote "I QUIT," in all caps, and signed his name.

"Here," he said, handing it to David.

"What's this?"

"My resignation letter. It's effective immediately. Good luck with Eden," he said and strode out through the door, already punching a number into his phone. "Jessie? I'm going to need Becky's address. I have a mistake to fix."

CHAPTER THIRTEEN

BECKY STEPPED BACK to admire the Christmas tree. Twinkling lights sparkled from its branches, highlighting the perfectly coordinated red and gold ornaments.

"It looks like something out of a store catalog," her mother said, a note of wistfulness in her voice.

"A little too perfect, huh?"

"No, I just wish you'd saved a little room for our family ornaments. I really love that snowman you made when you were five."

Her shoulders slumped. "I'm sorry, Mom, I was just trying to do something useful. I feel like such a mooch."

Her mom hadn't let her do anything since she'd arrived home. She didn't want any help cleaning. Wouldn't allow her to touch a pot or pan. And she refused to accept any money for her room and board—money Becky knew her parents could use.

The forced idleness was driving her batty.

"You're not a mooch. You're my daughter, recovering from a very recent heartbreak and trying to build a whole new life—while making a new life. Cut yourself some slack."

She sighed. "I'll try. It's just that I'm feeling itchy. I need to go back to work. I haven't had this long of a break between jobs since I was sixteen."

"I know. Give it time, Becky. The right opportunity will come along."

"I hope so. Can you bring me the other box of ornaments? I'll fix the tree."

As her mother disappeared into the basement Becky heard the muffled sound of her phone trilling from somewhere in the room.

"Oh, great. Where'd I put the damn thing now?" she muttered, lifting boxes and tossing pillows.

She finally found it, mushed between two couch cushions.

"Hello?" she said a little breathlessly.

"There you are. I was just getting ready to leave you a message."

"Oh, hey, Amy. What's up? Another car agency sniffing around?"

"Nope, I promised not to bother you with any more of those. This one's different."

"All right, I'm listening," Becky said.

"Well, it's a new agency. Pretty much brand-new."

"Uh-oh…"

"Now, hang on. They have some pretty big accounts. And not automotive, either."

"Which ones?"

"I'm not allowed to tell you. You have to sign a nondisclosure agreement first. But they said you're first on their list of candidates. Said they'd pay a premium if I could snag you."

"Hmm. That's flattering."

"It is. *Very.* Why don't you just go and see what they have to say? It could be just what you're looking for."

She looked over at her OCD tree and nodded. "All right. At the very least it will give me something to do."

Becky parked in front of a bright yellow Victorian house, checking the address one more time. Yep, this was where Amy had directed her to go.

Huh? It didn't look like any ad agency she'd ever seen. She had to admit that the surroundings were charming, though. It had the same vibe that all her favorite New York neighborhoods had—young and hip and full of life.

She shouldered her laptop bag and clacked up the carefully manicured walk. As she crossed the covered porch she noticed a small woodcut sign that read 'Trio' hanging from the wreath hook.

Definitely the right place, then.

She was about to ring the bell when a gawky pink-haired girl opened the door.

"You must be Becky," she said, blue eyes sparkling.

"I am. And you are…?"

"Izzie. I'm just a temp, but I'm hoping to convince the owner to keep me on," she said conspiratorially.

"Ah," Becky said, at a loss for words.

"Come on in," she said. "He's expecting you."

She stepped inside and handed Izzie her coat, taking a moment to check out her surroundings. The house looked fabulous—contemporary furnishings contrasting nicely with ornate woodwork and jewel-toned walls.

"It's this way," Izzie said, leading Becky into what must have once been the dining area but what was now a fully kitted-out conference room.

"Have a seat anywhere you like. He'll be right in."

Becky pulled out one of the cushy wood chairs and sat down, realizing she had no idea who she was about to interview with. No one had ever given her a name.

Oh, well. The mystery would be solved soon enough.

She fired up her laptop and was opening her online portfolio when she heard a familiar rumble.

"There you are. Detroit's hottest copywriter, in the flesh. Thank you for agreeing to meet with me."

Her head snapped up. *It couldn't be.*

It was.

Mark stood in the doorway, wearing a tailored black suit, looking even more delicious than she remembered.

Her emotions spun, unsure whether to settle on absolute fury or melting delight. She stood, fighting the urge to either hug or throttle him.

"M-Mark? What are you doing here?"

"This is my agency."

"Wait. What? No. You belong at SBD."

"Not anymore. I quit."

"You quit?" she asked, fury winning. "After I gave up everything for you? What the hell did you do that for?"

"I had to."

"Why? Did you lose the account?" Surely he couldn't have screwed up that badly that fast.

"No. I brought it with me."

She sank back down in her chair. "Okay, I am completely lost."

Mark stepped into the room and pulled down a white screen.

"Let me do this right," he said. "I put together a presentation to explain everything to you. Will you listen?"

Unable to speak, Becky nodded.

"Okay," he said, clicking a few buttons on his Mac. A picture of a sullen teenage boy filled the screen.

"Once upon a time there was a boy with a nasty attitude. He lived in a big house, and attended the most exclusive schools, but had the world's biggest stick up his ass. He had long ago decided his mother didn't love him, her illegitimate son, and nothing she did could change his mind."

He clicked forward to an image of a grinning Mark in a graduation cap and gown.

"He managed to graduate from college in spite of himself, and soon embarked on a career in the soulless world of advertising. He was quite good. Racked up lots of awards. And he managed to get through his twenties without ever having a real relationship."

He clicked forward to a shot of the famous Vegas sign.

"Then he went on a business trip and met a woman who would change his life forever. They spent only one night together, but by the time she left he was already falling in love. Not that he was capable of admitting it."

He flipped forward again to show the SBD sign.

"Then he got hired to work with and compete against the same phenomenal woman. Although he told himself not to get involved, he quickly did. They worked together, played together and won the account together. Somewhere along the way he fell head over heels, but still couldn't admit it to himself."

He clicked forward to a shot of a pregnant tummy.

"When she told him she was pregnant he reverted back to that sullen little boy and ran for the hills."

He clicked forward to David's headshot.

"Then the evil agency owner cooked up a plan to get rid of the girl. Both the girl and the boy fell for it, and before he knew it she was gone."

He clicked forward to a gray sky.

"Without her, his world fell apart. But it wasn't until he discovered the evil agency owner's dastardly plan that he managed to get rid of the stick still up his ass."

Another click and one of their Eden ad designs filled the screen.

"He submitted his resignation on a cocktail napkin and headed to the Eden company to tell them what he knew. Being decent people, they fired SBD and signed on the dotted line with the boy's as yet unnamed agency—on the condition that he find his better half."

He clicked forward to the yellow house.

"So here he is. Starting over. In Detroit. Betting that the woman he doesn't deserve will give him another chance with her heart and let him be her partner and her baby's daddy."

"Are you serious?" she whispered.

"Do I ever bet when I think I might lose?"

"I don't know," she said, her mind whirling. "This is all so sudden..."

"I have one more thing to show you," he said. "Will you come?"

She nodded and he led her up the ornate wooden staircase. He opened a door and stepped through to the sunny yellow room beyond.

"This is your office," he said. "And this," he went on, opening a door with a placard reading CEO, "is our baby's office."

It was a nursery, done in shades of green and yellow, complete with crib, rocking chair and changing table.

"My office is just over there," he said, pointing to a door on the far side of the room. He turned to her and smiled. "What do you think?"

She opened and closed her mouth, spinning in a slow circle in the middle of the room. "It's amazing," she breathed.

Mark crossed the room in two steps and got down on one knee, producing a diamond ring from his suit pocket.

"Becky, I'm ready to go all-in. I want us to be a family. Will you do me the honor of becoming my wife, partner and best friend?"

Becky thought her heart might explode with joy.

"Yes," she said. "Oh, yes."

Mark solemnly placed the ring on her left hand, then grinned up at her.

"I bet I know what you want me to do now."

"What?" she asked, smiling through the tears streaming down her face.

"This," he said, rising to take her in his arms and claim her lips.

Becky looped her arms around his neck and kissed him back with everything she had.

"You win again, Magic Man," she murmured. "But do you know what I want more than anything right now?"

"No. What?"

"For you to take me to bed."

"I don't have any beds here yet. Will a desk do?"

"Splendidly." She grinned.

He swooped her up into his arms and carried her over the threshold into his office.

"God, I missed you, Gorgeous Girl."

"Prove it," she said.

And so he did.

EPILOGUE

BECKY WAS JUST clicking through to her final PowerPoint slide when a baby's cry echoed through the monitor placed discreetly under the conference room table.

She grinned and nudged the power switch to the Off position with her toe.

"And that's how we'll make the Eden campaign the advertising darling of the new year, fueling New Year's Resolutions across the country."

As applause broke out around the crowded conference table Izzie poked her head through the white-paneled door.

"He needs to be fed," Izzie said in a stage whisper.

Becky motioned for her to come in and gathered the baby into her arms.

"If you have any questions, Mark can field them," she said, moving to the comfy rocker tucked behind a folding screen in the corner.

She listened, baby nestled at her breast, as Mark swung into action. In no time he had sweet talked the Eden people into spending even more money with their tiny agency in the next year.

Trio's future was secured.

When they were finally gone, Mark plopped down on the rocker's ottoman and stroked the baby's cheek.

"Well, I'm glad that's over," he said.

"Were you worried they wouldn't sign?" she asked.

"No, not really. I just want to move on to the day's big event."

"Big event? I know I've been preoccupied," she said, indicating the baby nestled on her chest, "but I thought that meeting was our last piece of client business until after the holidays."

"It was. This has nothing to do with business."

"Then what is it?"

Mark grinned. "It's a surprise. Do you trust me?"

"You know I do," Becky said.

"Good. Then I need you to head up the back staircase into your office and do whatever Izzie tells you to do. Okay?"

"Okaaayyy… I guess," Becky said. "Now?"

"Yep. Now," he said, pulling her to her feet.

"What about Alex?"

"I'll take care of Alex. Hand him over," Mark said, holding his arms out for the baby.

Becky kissed his soft head, then reluctantly gave him to Mark. Even after five months of life as a mom it still amazed her how in love she was with her baby.

"He just ate, so he's going to need a diaper—"

"I know," said Mark.

"And he needs to do some tummy time…"

"Got it. Just go."

"Okay. If you're sure…?"

Mark sighed. "Becky. You're just going to be upstairs. I've got this."

She realized she was being a bit ridiculous. "All right, I'm going," she grumbled, and headed for the kitchen door.

When she opened her office door, she was shocked to see four different people rushing about, setting up mirrors and plugging in hair appliances.

"What on earth is going on here?" she asked.

Izzie's pink-haired head popped up from behind her desk, plug in hand.

"Oh, there you are! We're on a mission to doll you up. Now, hurry up and get in here. There's not much time!"

"Time before what? I'm so confused," Becky moaned.

Izzie grabbed her by the hand and pulled her behind a screen that had been set up in the corner.

"Don't worry about it, boss lady." Izzie grinned. "You're going to love it. Now, just relax and go with the flow."

Realizing she had no real choice in the matter, Becky nodded. "All right, I'll try."

"Good," Izzie said, unzipping a dress bag. "You can start by stripping down to your skivvies. We need to make sure this fits you."

Becky gasped when she saw the confection Izzie was holding. It was a full-length evening gown made of red velvet. Gold and red beaded embroidery sparkled at the bodice and traced a delicate path down to the hip of the A-line skirt, then flowed along the hem. Cap sleeves finished it off.

"It's beautiful," she breathed.

"It'll look even better on you," Izzie said. "Now. come on—off with your clothes."

Two hours later Becky was staring at her reflection in a full-length mirror, not recognizing the gorgeous woman staring back at her, when there was a knock on the door.

"Come in," she called, not bothering to turn around.

"Wow. If that's what having a baby does for your body, sign me up," a familiar voice said.

Becky whirled, unable to believe her ears. "Jessie!" she shrieked when she saw her beloved redheaded friend grinning at her from the doorway. "Jessie, what are you doing here?"

"Oh, you know," she said. "I was just in the neighborhood, so I thought I'd stop by…"

"You are such a liar." Becky laughed, throwing her arms

around her friend. "But I don't care. I'm just so glad to see you!"

Jessie squeezed her back. "Me, too, lady. Me, too. But, hey, we better be careful. I don't want to muss that gorgeous gown you're wearing."

Becky disentangled herself and did a little twirl.

"I know. Isn't it amazing? But I have no idea why I'm wearing it."

"I do. And so will you in a few minutes," Jessie said. "But first I need to freshen up. Izzie? What have you got for me?"

Izzie dragged her behind the screen and Becky went back to gawking at herself in the mirror. Her blond hair was swept up with an elegant mass of sequined hairpins, artfully crafted curls framing her face. The makeup artist had made her emerald eyes look huge, and she was sure her lips were nowhere near that plump.

The dress emphasized her newfound curves, and for the first time since Alex was born she felt beautiful.

Tears welled in her eyes. She had no idea what Mark was planning, but she owed him big for helping her feel like a woman again.

Just then Jessie's faced popped up behind her shoulder. "Hey, hey, hey—no crying allowed! You're wearing way too much mascara for that."

Becky smiled, wiping at the corner of her eye as she turned. Jessie had changed into an elegant green cocktail dress, with the same gold embroidery flashing around the knee-length hem.

"Wow. You clean up good. Wait a minute..." she said, realization dawning. "That looks like a bridesmaid's dress. But we haven't even begun planning the wedding. It's supposed to be in June!"

Just then the lilting sound of a harp playing her favorite hymn floated up to her ears.

"Isn't it?"

Jessie just winked and peeked her head out through the door.

"Mark? We're ready for you!"

Seconds later Mark stood in the doorway, wearing a tuxedo. "Hey, babe." He grinned. "You ready to get married?"

Becky sat down heavily in her chair. "But I thought—I mean, we'd always talked about June!" Not that she'd done anything to put plans in motion.

Mark crossed the room and kneeled down in front of her. "I know, Becky, I know. But it was a year ago today, right here in this house, when we became a family. I thought it only fitting that we make it legal in the same place. Besides," he said, kissing her fingers, "I don't want to wait another six months. I want the whole world to know you're mine *now.* Becky Logan, will you do me the honor of becoming my wife today?"

Becky dabbed at her eyes again, holding back the tears by force of will alone. "Of course I will," she said, joy fizzing in her veins.

"Good," he said. "Then let's do this thing."

From the hallway, Izzie called, "Hit it, guys!" and a string quartet launched into the "Wedding March."

Becky put her hand in the crook of Mark's arm. "Let's do it."

Mark stood in front of Becky's childhood priest, listening to the sermon with half an ear as he gazed at the beautiful woman who had agreed to be his wife. Even the glow of the twinkling white Christmas lights that sparkled around them paled in comparison to the joy emanating from her.

To think he had almost missed out on all of this. Now that their baby had arrived he couldn't imagine life without him. Not to mention his mother.

Becky caught him staring and smiled, love shining from her eyes. "I love you," she mouthed silently.

"I love you, too," he mouthed back.

"If I can get these lovebirds to stop mooning over each other for a minute, we'll get to the real reason you're all here," the priest said, breaking into their silent communion. "But first let me ask all who are gathered here an important question. Is there anyone here who objects to this marriage? If so, speak now or forever hold your peace."

Silence fell, making the sudden outraged shriek from their baby's miniature lungs echo all the louder.

"We'll assume that's his way of objecting to his place on the sidelines and not to his parents' matrimony," the priest joked as the room erupted with laughter.

"Well, let's fix that." Becky giggled, and motioned for her mother to bring the baby forward. "After all, he's part of this family, too."

Once he was settled on her hip, the angry cries turned into contented coos.

"All right. Now that we're all settled," the priest said, "do you, Becky, take this man to be your lawfully wedded husband, to care for him and keep him, in sickness and in health, in good times and in bad, all the days of your life?"

"I do," she said softly, and Mark's heart swelled.

"And do you, Mark, take this woman to be your lawfully wedded wife, to care for her and keep her, in sickness and in health, in good times and in bad, all the days of your life?"

"You bet I do," he said, putting his whole heart into every word.

"Then it is my honor to proclaim you husband and wife. Mark, you may kiss the bride."

Mark gathered her to him, careful not to dislodge the baby from her hip. "Now you're mine," he whispered, and pressed his lips to hers, silently communicating his joy.

"I always was," she whispered against his mouth.

Alex chortled happily as they broke apart, and, laughing, Mark bent to kiss his cheek.

"Ladies and gentlemen, I am overjoyed to present to you Mr. and Mrs. Powers!"

The small crowd rose to its feet and applauded.

Looking around at the sea of happy faces, Mark felt at peace. Love might be a gamble, but he was pretty sure he'd hit the jackpot.

* * * * *

Mills & Boon® Hardback

September 2014

ROMANCE

The Housekeeper's Awakening	Sharon Kendrick
More Precious than a Crown	Carol Marinelli
Captured by the Sheikh	Kate Hewitt
A Night in the Prince's Bed	Chantelle Shaw
Damaso Claims His Heir	Annie West
Changing Constantinou's Game	Jennifer Hayward
The Ultimate Revenge	Victoria Parker
Tycoon's Temptation	Trish Morey
The Party Dare	Anne Oliver
Sleeping with the Soldier	Charlotte Phillips
All's Fair in Lust & War	Amber Page
Dressed to Thrill	Bella Frances
Interview with a Tycoon	Cara Colter
Her Boss by Arrangement	Teresa Carpenter
In Her Rival's Arms	Alison Roberts
Frozen Heart, Melting Kiss	Ellie Darkins
After One Forbidden Night...	Amber McKenzie
Dr Perfect on Her Doorstep	Lucy Clark

MEDICAL

A Secret Shared...	Marion Lennox
Flirting with the Doc of Her Dreams	Janice Lynn
The Doctor Who Made Her Love Again	Susan Carlisle
The Maverick Who Ruled Her Heart	Susan Carlisle

0814GEN STD HB

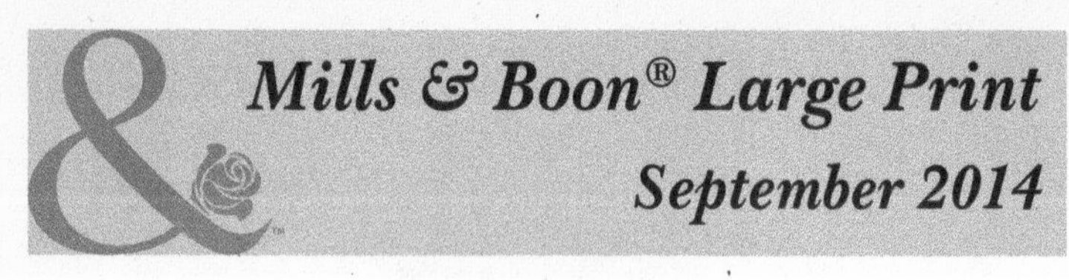

ROMANCE

The Only Woman to Defy Him	Carol Marinelli
Secrets of a Ruthless Tycoon	Cathy Williams
Gambling with the Crown	Lynn Raye Harris
The Forbidden Touch of Sanguardo	Julia James
One Night to Risk it All	Maisey Yates
A Clash with Cannavaro	Elizabeth Power
The Truth About De Campo	Jennifer Hayward
Expecting the Prince's Baby	Rebecca Winters
The Millionaire's Homecoming	Cara Colter
The Heir of the Castle	Scarlet Wilson
Twelve Hours of Temptation	Shoma Narayanan

HISTORICAL

Unwed and Unrepentant	Marguerite Kaye
Return of the Prodigal Gilvry	Ann Lethbridge
A Traitor's Touch	Helen Dickson
Yield to the Highlander	Terri Brisbin
Return of the Viking Warrior	Michelle Styles

MEDICAL

Waves of Temptation	Marion Lennox
Risk of a Lifetime	Caroline Anderson
To Play with Fire	Tina Beckett
The Dangers of Dating Dr Carvalho	Tina Beckett
Uncovering Her Secrets	Amalie Berlin
Unlocking the Doctor's Heart	Susanne Hampton

0814 GEN STD LP

Mills & Boon® Hardback
October 2014

ROMANCE

An Heiress for His Empire	Lucy Monroe
His for a Price	Caitlin Crews
Commanded by the Sheikh	Kate Hewitt
The Valquez Bride	Melanie Milburne
The Uncompromising Italian	Cathy Williams
Prince Hafiz's Only Vice	Susanna Carr
A Deal Before the Altar	Rachael Thomas
Rival's Challenge	Abby Green
The Party Starts at Midnight	Lucy King
Your Bed or Mine?	Joss Wood
Turning the Good Girl Bad	Avril Tremayne
Breaking the Bro Code	Stefanie London
The Billionaire in Disguise	Soraya Lane
The Unexpected Honeymoon	Barbara Wallace
A Princess by Christmas	Jennifer Faye
His Reluctant Cinderella	Jessica Gilmore
One More Night with Her Desert Prince...	Jennifer Taylor
From Fling to Forever	Avril Tremayne

MEDICAL

It Started with No Strings...	Kate Hardy
Flirting with Dr Off-Limits	Robin Gianna
Dare She Date Again?	Amy Ruttan
The Surgeon's Christmas Wish	Annie O'Neil

ROMANCE

Ravelli's Defiant Bride	Lynne Graham
When Da Silva Breaks the Rules	Abby Green
The Heartbreaker Prince	Kim Lawrence
The Man She Can't Forget	Maggie Cox
A Question of Honour	Kate Walker
What the Greek Can't Resist	Maya Blake
An Heir to Bind Them	Dani Collins
Becoming the Prince's Wife	Rebecca Winters
Nine Months to Change His Life	Marion Lennox
Taming Her Italian Boss	Fiona Harper
Summer with the Millionaire	Jessica Gilmore

HISTORICAL

Scars of Betrayal	Sophia James
Scandal's Virgin	Louise Allen
An Ideal Companion	Anne Ashley
Surrender to the Viking	Joanna Fulford
No Place for an Angel	Gail Whitiker

MEDICAL

200 Harley Street: Surgeon in a Tux	Carol Marinelli
200 Harley Street: Girl from the Red Carpet	Scarlet Wilson
Flirting with the Socialite Doc	Melanie Milburne
His Diamond Like No Other	Lucy Clark
The Last Temptation of Dr Dalton	Robin Gianna
Resisting Her Rebel Hero	Lucy Ryder

0914 GEN STD LP